How could she have forgotten so easily?

Nicole went rigid with shame. Lang's disturbing mouth lifted from hers when he felt her resistance.

"What's wrong, Nicky?" he asked, puzzled.

"Nothing." She eased herself out of his arms. "I stupidly, but only temporarily, forgot my own well-founded conclusions, that's all," she replied through trembling lips.

He made no attempt to stop her, but his eyes narrowed alertly. "Which are?"

"That you're no different from any other man," she retorted. "That you're all natural two-timers. But you needn't think I'm going along with it. Not me!"

She stormed out, slamming the door. The most galling part of the whole episode had been her unqualified surrender to Lang's lovemaking. How humiliating if she had inadvertently revealed her real feelings for him!

Across the Great Divide

by

KERRY ALLYNE

Harlequin Books

TORONTO • LONDON • NEW YORK • AMSTERDAM
SYDNEY • HAMBURG • PARIS • STOCKHOLM

Original hardcover edition published in 1979
by Mills & Boon Limited

ISBN 0-373-02323-5

Harlequin edition published April 1980

Printed in U.S.A.

CHAPTER ONE

THE taxi driver, a burly man in his late forties, took another glance in the rear vision mirror to scan the features of his young passenger and wondered again about the cause of that tautly set expression. Man trouble more than likely, he decided, flicking on his indicating light and turning off the main road into a residential street. As he had three daughters of a similar age the signs weren't altogether new to him. It was a pity though, he continued to himself, because she was an attractive little thing. Not beautiful exactly, but very easy on the eyes all the same, with that heart-shaped gamine face.

By the look of her, dressed in a brightly printed gown of floating chiffon, he presumed she had been at a party, and had been surprised to find she was the only passenger after answering a call for a cab to that large white brick house in Dee Why. The fact that she had hurried out to the car alone carrying an overnight bag immediately he had pulled up only served to convince him that his deduction was correct. This particular Saturday night hadn't ended pleasantly for at least one pair of lovers!

In response to his passenger's huskily given direc-

5

tions some minutes later he drew to a halt before a small block of plain-looking apartments and waited while she extracted the fare from her purse. His offer to carry her bag to the door was rejected with a low, half smiled, 'No thank you,' together with a brief dismissing movement of one slender hand, and then she was out of the cab and heading quickly for the entrance to the building where a single light gleamed dully in the surrounding darkness. With an easy-going shrug he eased the vehicle back into gear and moved out from the curb. A phone call from her boy-friend in the morning would probably have it all made up between them in no time.

But Nicole Lockwood knew differently, and as she made her way up the flight of stairs to the second floor apartment she shared with her father and elder sister her steps slowed and long-subdued tears began stabbing at her eyelids. For over a year now she had dated Jerome Schafer and it had been generally accepted by both their families and their friends that the two of them would marry as soon as he had fulfilled his ambition to be made a partner in the firm of solicitors for whom he worked. Rothwell, Smedley and Poulton were a distinguished firm among Sydney's legal circles, and no one could have been prouder than Nicole when Jerome had rung her the day before to say that his long-awaited admittance to the hallowed inner circle had finally become a reality and that his parents were throwing a party in celebration.

There had been no hint then of what was to come, nor on their journey to his home earlier that evening. Not even on sight of her bag which she had packed automatically because she always stayed the night when the Schafers had a party to save Jerome the long trip of bringing her home in the early hours of the morning. No, it had been left to Deirdre Rothwell's presence, the senior partner's willowy blonde daughter, to drag the wool from her eyes and allow her to see just how ambitious Jerome really was. He might have been telling her, Nicole, just how much he loved her for the past fourteen months, but it was Deirdre he was going to marry. Apparently hard work hadn't been the only method he'd employed to ensure that tempting fourth partnership wasn't offered elsewhere!

At first Nicole had only been slightly annoyed when the other girl began commandeering Jerome's attention during the evening. Then she had caught snatches of conversation the other guests were making regarding the anticipated nuptials between the pair of them and with burning flares of indignation colouring her cheeks she had done a little commandeering herself and managed to get Jerome alone for a few minutes while Deirdre was otherwise occupied for once.

'From the amount of time you're spending with

her I'm not surprised everyone thinks Deirdre's the girl you're going to marry,' she had laughed lightly. 'I know she's the boss's daughter and all that, but do you really have to dance attendance on her *all* night?'

'I'm sorry, Nicky, but it's expected of me under the —er—circumstances,' he had replied, without quite returning her gaze.

'Because you're now her father's partner?'

'No ...' He had stopped to clear his throat uneasily, his face distinctly reddening. 'Because—because I've asked her to—to be my wife. I was going to. . . .'

'Your *wife*!' she had burst in, stunned. 'But how could you when we're ... when you and I were ...?'

'But there was never anything definite between us, was there, Nicky?' he'd interrupted quickly. 'I mean, nothing was settled, was it? We hadn't put it into so many words.'

Nicole could remember shaking her head in a state of shock and feeling as if her whole secure world had suddenly disintegrated. That he should pretend there had been nothing permanent in their relationship was bad enough, but to break it to her at such a gathering and in such a way was unbelievable!

'As I started to say before, I was going to tell you. . . .'

'Then why didn't you?' she had demanded, pride coming to her aid in not allowing him to guess how much his desertion hurt. 'Why wait and let me find out this way?'

'Because I didn't have a chance to see you before and I didn't think it right to tell you over the phone.'

'You think this is better?' Her expression had become openly scornful.

'At least it gives me the opportunity to try and explain. To try and make you understand why.'

Nicole had a strong suspicion she knew that already!

'And what was wrong with saying something when you picked me up earlier?' she asked then. 'Or didn't you think that would have been convincing enough?' Tears had started into her wide-spaced eyes, turning them a misty blue. 'How could you have let me come here expecting to stay the night as if everything was the same as usual when you knew very well I was bound to find out about you and Deirdre? My God, just what kind of man are you, Jerome?'

'Look, I'm sorry, but I really didn't mean it to turn out this way,' he had promptly tried to vindicate himself. 'I just thought that....'

'Being an out-and-out coward, it would be a whole lot more convenient if you left matters to follow their own course and consequently save yourself the trouble of going into lengthy excuses before it became absolutely necessary!'

'No! How could you think that?'

'How?' she had laughed bitterly. 'By your making it so easy, I guess.'

Further explanations and apologies had followed

but, not surprisingly, Nicole hadn't evinced much interest in any of them. Her sole desire had been to leave the party as soon as possible. Painful though the acknowledgment might have been, there was no evading the fact that she had been summarily but decidedly jilted, and she had no option but to accept the rejection by showing as little of the pain and bewilderment she was feeling as she could.

On reaching the landing of the flats she wiped the heavy wetness from her lashes with her fingertips and glanced at the small gold watch clasped about her wrist before unlocking the door to the apartment. Thank heavens it was after twelve, she sighed. Both her father and sister would be well asleep by now and their barrage of questions as to why she had come home instead of staying overnight at the Schafers' could be postponed until the morning. At the moment she was in no mood, or condition, to answer any searching enquiries.

Closing the door softly behind her, Nicole crept through the lounge in the dark. It was only a single-bedroomed flat and her father slept on the convertible sofa in the lounge while her sister Cynthia and herself shared the double bed in the other room—a temporary arrangement they had made do with since moving into the apartment a few weeks ago as Cynthia was to be married the following weekend and her father would be leaving to take up a position in the country the week after.

Born and raised in the bush, Bryce Lockwood had only moved to the city when his wife died—Nicole had been six at the time and Cynthia ten—in order for them to experience a woman's touch in their lives in the form of their maternal grandmother. For the girls it had been an unworrying transplant, but for Bryce it had been a sacrifice, willingly made, but a forfeiture nonetheless. He was and always would be a bushman at heart and since his daughters had become of an age to take care of themselves competently now that their grandmother had passed away, his thoughts had been claimed more and more frequently by the idea of returning to his own milieu.

Both girls had been aware of his longings in this regard and, in fact, they had been the ones to pressure him into applying for the post of stock overseer on a property in the north-west which had been advertised some weeks ago. Doubting that he would be successful after so many years spent in the city, Bryce had attended an interview at the agents' offices with more than a little trepidation—a circumstance which made his eventual acceptance for the position all the more pleasurable.

Inside the compact bathroom Nicole stripped off her clothes, washed quickly, and slipped on the short red and white checked nightdress she had packed in her overnight bag. There was less likelihood of her waking Cynthia if she was dressed before entering the bedroom. Passing the wall mirror as she made for the door, she stopped and stared disconsolately at her wan reflection.

Even without a lucrative partnership as an added bonus, how could straight light brown hair, childishly wide blue eyes, a freckle-spattered snub nose and an impudent-looking mouth hope to compete with Deirdre Rothwell's svelte blonde beauty? Her figure might have been better proportioned but, at five feet four, even that could never aspire to the tall, slim elegance the other girl exemplified so effortlessly.

Cynthia could have made a contest of it—she was tall too. But, of course, her sister also had the benefit of the beautifully classic features which had made her so in demand as a photographic model for the last six years, as well as her rich brown hair and dark expressive eyes which would serve her outstandingly in any company, blonde or otherwise! No, it was just cute little Nicky—she didn't even rate the more dignified 'Nicole' from most people—who was forever doomed to be typed as the girl next door for the rest of her life! Perhaps it wasn't so surprising that Jerome had preferred....

She bit hard on her lip to still its trembling, her eyes beginning to water traitorously again as she flicked off the light before opening the door and tiptoeing through to the bedroom. Oh, why had that damned partnership had to mean so much to Jerome? Why couldn't he have been satisfied with the position he already had? She couldn't have loved him any the less if he hadn't risen any further within the hierarchy. Why had it had to end this way? With an aching pain in the region of her heart that was threatening to tear her in two, and a dull apathy for all the empty tomorrows that were still to come? Why, oh, why?

With the blinds drawn it was only possible to tell Cynthia's whereabouts by her steady rhythmical breathing and Nicole slid gently between the sheets, keeping well over to her side of the bed but clenching her hands when the other figure moved unexpectedly, then releasing them again with a tremulous sigh as her sister's breathing resumed its even cadence. Closing her eyes tightly, Nicole determinedly sought oblivion as the only means of ejecting Jerome from her thoughts and his image from her mind. But only when exhausted sleep finally overtook her was she to be rid of the hurtful pictures, for then they turned into an enchanting fantasy wherein he responded to her crying of his name with strong arms securing her protectively close against a broad chest and thrilling lips, exacting a return she was all too eager to give.

When morning came she left the realms of euphoria behind slowly, reluctantly, her gold-tipped lashes fluttering open drowsily and her slender form stretching lethargically. Only half awake, she could still feel Jerome's arms around her and the smooth hard skin of his shoulder beneath her cheek as she lay curled against him. It all seemed so *real*, she sighed regretfully. She could almost bring herself to believe that *was* Jerome she could feel with her trailing fingertips, except that.... Except that *was* firm living flesh she was touching, and Jerome wasn't that muscular!

Full consciousness hit her like a sudden spray of freezing water and her eyes flew wide open in panic as a large hand abruptly covered her mouth, shutting off her first startled cry, and she found herself staring into a totally unknown but extremely male countenance.

'Before you start screaming blue murder, allow me to introduce myself,' he grinned down at her lazily, white teeth gleaming against a deeply tanned skin. 'I'm Lang Jamieson, your father's new employer—I presume you are Bryce's youngest daughter, Nicole? —and as neither you nor your sister was expected to be using the bed last night your father kindly offered it to me to save a trip back to my hotel in town. Okay?'

Nicole nodded. His explanation had relieved some of her worries, but certainly not all of them, and as soon as he removed his hand from her mouth she struggled furiously away from his disturbing contact and into a sitting position, her clutching fingers dragging the sheet about her in an attempt to shield the transparency of her attire.

'Well, you might at least have had the decency to

inform me immediately I got into the bed, Mr Jamieson,' she retorted hotly, still remembering with embarrassment the imprint of his lithe frame pressed against her own. 'You must have known I thought it was my sister beside me.'

He clasped his hands behind his head and leant back against his pillow leisurely, tawny eyes mocking. 'You don't say?' he drawled. 'Correct me if I'm wrong, but I gained the impression I was substituting for someone called Jerome ... not Cynthia.'

Nicole swallowed agonisingly as realisation flooded through her. 'You mean, it—it wasn't a dream? That it was *you* who was ... it was your....' She stopped and glared at him contemptuously. 'And like all men you were only too willing to turn the opportunity to your advantage, I suppose!'

'Quite the reverse, I would have said,' he returned sardonically. 'Remember, *I* wasn't the one having trouble sleeping, kitten. I just did us both a favour by making it possible for you to do likewise.'

'That was big of you!' she jeered. 'It didn't occur to you that under those circumstances I might have preferred a restless night?'

'Mmm, the thought did cross my mind, but as you seemed all too inclined to go along with the substitution, who was I to disappoint the lady?' he queried with a deliberately reminiscent smile that had Nicole's temper flaring uncontrollably.

'Why, you—you self-centred braggart, you could

never take the place of Jerome!' she hurled back at him scathingly, her breasts heaving. 'At least he wouldn't resort to such low tactics in order to keep a girl in *his* bed!'

A hand snaked out to twine roughly within her silky hair and before Nicole knew what was happening she was flat on her back with a grim face only inches from hers as he leant over her.

'And you'd better get your facts right before you start directing accusations of that nature at me, you peevish little cat!' he rasped. 'You appeared in need of solace last night and I gave it to you, that's all ... nothing else! Believe me, weeping females have never been my idea of desirable sleeping partners!' He released her dismissively.

'Then get out of my bed!'

His dark head inclined downwards in sarcastic acknowledgment. 'Gladly.'

As he started to match his actions to his words Nicole turned her back on him, only a deeply rooted courtesy making her divulge woodenly, 'There's a towelling shave coat of Dad's in the wardrobe you can use if you want to shower before getting dressed.'

'Thanks.'

His answer was as stiff as her advice had been and a few minutes later he crossed her line of vision heading for the door with the navy blue coat belted about his lean waist. With his hand on the knob he swung back to face her, brows lifting ironically.

'Shall I tell your father we shared the bed, or would you prefer to break the news yourself?' he asked.

As thoughts of Jerome crowded dismally into her mind Nicole returned his look with bitter eyes. 'Whichever suits your convenience, Mr Jamieson. That *is* the accepted male prerogative, isn't it?'

Annoyingly, he laughed, and it was a thoroughly pleasant, masculine sound. 'Never mind, Nicky, you'll get over it. These things fade with time.'

'Oh, why don't you get lost?' she snapped irritably, and flounced over in the bed to present him with a view of her honey-gold back again. 'Right at the moment I need your trite little pieces of wisdom about as much as a fish needs water-wings!'

'No, I'd agree you need something far stronger to shake you out of the depths of self-pity you're in danger of sinking into,' he retorted disparagingly. 'Either that, or your father is going to be mighty thankful to leave you behind in two weeks' time.'

Nicole whirled to face him once more with a withering rejection on her lips, but he had already left the room and she subsided on to her back with a sigh. Surely she was entitled to feel just a little sorry for herself in the circumstances? It wasn't an emotion she usually cared to indulge but, on this occasion, she did consider she had reason. To be jilted at all was bad enough, but to have done it in such a fashion had been not only weak-kneed but positively callous as well!

As for her father—well, she hoped he would prove a little more understanding than this Lang Jamieson apparently was. By the sound of it, his efforts at comforting had only been motivated by a wish to settle her so he could go back to sleep himself. The heartless, unfeeling brute! What she wouldn't give to see him in the same position one day! Not that it was very likely, of course, because after today she didn't expect to see him again—something she wouldn't be losing any sleep over. Besides, she mused grudgingly, he really hadn't come across as the type of man a woman would voluntarily let go once she had attracted him. In retrospect, now she came to think of it, he was quite a good-looking, powerfully built specimen of the male of the species. She supposed him to be in his early thirties—certainly much younger than she had expected her parent's employer to be—with dark waving hair and a pair of unusually coloured gold-flecked eyes. His nose was straight and uncomplicated within the clean hard lines of his face where a decisively square chin silently predicted the man's forceful personality, and he possessed a firmly shaped mouth which she knew from experience could curve into a heart-shaking smile.

She groaned and closed her eyes tightly. All her analysis had succeeded in doing was to induce a comparison with Jerome—and the two men were as different as chalk and cheese. The infinitely male and mahogany-skinned Lang Jamieson was too overwhelming a character in contrast to Jerome's light-haired and blue-eyed slimness.

When she judged she had allowed him enough time to be finished with the bathroom, Nicole emerged into the lounge room cautiously, knowing she had an interested interrogation to face from her father regarding her unexpected return home, but hoping to ward it off until after Lang Jamieson's departure. She had no wish for him to be a witness to the whole humliliating narration.

Sunday morning breakfast was normally a casual meal in the Lockwood household with each of them preparing their own when they felt like it, but as they had a guest with them this weekend her father was already laying the table for three in the nook off the kitchen when Nicole crossed swiftly to the bathroom, and he saw her before she could dart inside.

'Lang's been telling me how you unknowingly shared the bed last night,' he called after her with a frown. 'Didn't you even put the bedside light on when you came in?'

Nicole swept her long hair back over her shoulder, shrugged, and forced a rueful smile on to her lips.

'If I had, we wouldn't be having this conversation,' she quipped. 'But it was late when I got back and I didn't want to wake anyone. It never occurred to me it wouldn't be Cynthia in the bedroom.' Her gaze turned curious. 'Where is she, anyway?'

'Oh, Clark called her after you'd left,' Bryce relayed offhandedly. 'Apparently he had a late assignment for some work down the coast and she decided to go with him and make a weekend of it.'

'I see,' Nicole nodded.

As well as having been her photographer for the last three years, Clark Rutherford was also the man Cynthia would be marrying the following Saturday. But before her father could return to events closer at hand Nicole slipped hastily into the bathroom and slid the lock across with a sigh. At least she had managed to gain a brief respite!

That was all it was though, because immediately she left the room after showering and dressing in a pale pink flared skirt and a white cotton crocheted top, he had another question ready.

'Why did you come home last night, Nicky?' he asked. 'I thought you intended to stay overnight at the Schafers' as usual.'

'I did,' she replied awkwardly, keeping her eyes on his solid figure so her gaze couldn't connect with that of Lang Jamieson as he sat at the table watching her closely. 'But there was a—um—change of plans, so I came home instead.'

'He will still be coming to see you today, though?'

Reaching into the cupboard for the frying pan, she merely gave a quick shake of her head. 'No, not now,' she answered throatily and chewed at her lip as the hurtful words "or ever" flashed through her mind. 'Why, did you want to see him about something?'

'Only about the lease on this place,' he advised heavily. 'You know I don't like some of the clauses written into it and I thought I'd have a word with him to see if something couldn't be done regarding the one concerning eviction. With your sister married, and me gone, I've had strong reservations about the landlord being able to put you out on only a few days' notice. It's not that easy to find a decent flat in such a short time these days.'

Nicole began dropping sausages and bacon into the pan and sent him a wry smile.

'Oh, come on, Dad, I'm twenty-one years old, you don't have to worry about me. Anyway, on the rent I can afford to pay I doubt I could get a place with a longer eviction clause.'

'Hardly a reassuring thought for your father to take with him,' interposed Lang Jamieson smoothly, and received a furious glare from a pair of sparkling blue eyes for his interference.

Bryce, however, seemed grateful to have someone seconding his opinion.

'That's it in a nutshell!' he exclaimed. 'If it wasn't for the fact that you and Jerome are expected to make an announcement shortly, I'd say to hell with it and persuade you to come west with me.'

'And what would I do out there?' she laughed lightly in an attempt to direct his attention from the more personal. 'A swimming instructress would be a little out of place in the bush, don't you think?'

'There *are* towns on the other side of the ranges,' Lang reminded her promptly, sardonically. 'As a matter of fact I was only telling your father last night —after he mentioned your occupation—that we've just built a new pool in Nullegai and are looking for someone with your qualifications.'

'Well, you shouldn't have much trouble,' she retorted sweetly before her father started getting ideas. 'There are plenty of us around.'

'But not with such a good reason as you for moving that far away from the city.' A pause and then he frowned as if he had just remembered something. 'Oh, but I was forgetting, you have a definite reason for staying in Sydney, don't you? I gather from Bryce that you're anticipating following your sister to the altar in ... how long?' he queried so innocently that Nicole could quite cheerfully have broken the eggs over his head instead of into the pan.

The miserable heel! She suspected he knew damned well there was no such plan in the future for her now. She bent her head so her hair fell forward to curtain her face from view and replied stiffly:

'That decision is another of the privileges which belong to the male, Mr Jamieson, as I'm sure you already know only too well.'

'Hey, that doesn't sound like my little girl.' Her father put a brawny arm around her shoulders and hugged her close. 'What's wrong, love? Did you and Jerome have an argument last night?'

She would have been happy if that was all it had been!

'No, not really,' she evaded without looking at him as unwanted tears spilled on to her lashes.

'No, she's just crying because there's something in her eye.'

Oh, shut up, damn you, just shut up! Nicole screamed at Lang inwardly, although the blazing look she gave him said it for her just as effectively. Then her father was turning her face up to his with a gentle hand and his dark brown eyes, so like Cynthia's, were roaming speculatively over her flushed features.

'You never know, I might even be able to help if you told me what was troubling you,' he offered quietly.

Nicole dashed away the tears with the back of her hand and gazed up at him with tremulous affection. Poor Dad! Since Nanna died he had often found himself at something of a loss as to how best to cope with the various problems his daughters brought home. But no matter how hard he tried she didn't think there was anything he could do to help with this one.

'There's not a great deal to tell,' she smiled wistfully. 'Jerome and I have—have broken up, that's all.'

'That's *all*! But I thought....' He stopped, and started again. 'But why? Everything seemed fine when you left here yesterday.'

'Yes, well, that's the way it goes sometimes,' she shrugged as indifferently as possible while scooping the food on to a serving dish which she placed on the table so they could help themselves. 'He—we....' Oh, what the hell was she trying to hide? Lang Jamieson already knew—or guessed—what had happened, didn't he? 'Apparently Jerome's going to marry Deirdre Rothwell.'

'Rothwell!' Bryce picked up the name immediately. 'Of Rothwell, Smedley and Poulton?'

'The same.'

'So that's how he managed to obtain his partnership so quickly. The hypocritical bastard!' he denounced grimly. 'So why couldn't he have told you when he rang during the week, or before you left for the party?'

'I don't think he knew quite how to put it,' she grimaced as she took a seat at the table and dropped some bread into the toaster.

Pulling out a chair opposite their guest, Bryce gave a disparaging snort.

'I'm not surprised!' he muttered in an ominous and disgusted undertone. 'To think that all the time he was seeing you he was currying favour by ingratiating himself with his boss's daughter. I could wring his damned devious neck!'

'At least it solves your most worrying problem,' Lang inserted helpfully, and had two frowning faces swinging towards him. One very suspiciously.

'How's that?' Bryce questioned.

'Well, you've only just finished saying how much you disliked the idea of leaving Nicole on her own here, and now there's no need to,' he smiled cheerfully and brought forth his trump card. 'Especially since there's a readymade job waiting for her in Nullegai.'

So that was why he had gone to such lengths to bring her split with Jerome out into the open, Nicole fumed. They needed a swimming instructress for their new pool and she, very conveniently, fitted the bill! Well, she had news for him ... she wasn't buying!

'As much as I appreciate your magnanimous efforts to arrange my life for me, Mr Jamieson, I'm afraid I'm going to have to disappoint you. You see,' she sent him a deceptively sweet look from beneath her lashes, 'I already happen to have a perfectly good job here which I have no intention of leaving ... and certainly not in order to incarcerate myself in the middle of nowhere!'

Lang's eyes smouldered with a contemptuous fire. 'Because you're secretly nursing the hope that Don Juan might, in time, come to reconsider his choice?'

'Oh, no, not because of that—never because of that,' Nicole took pleasure in informing him disdainfully. 'I've learnt my lesson where men are concerned. They can find some other poor female to practise their two-faced wiles on in future.'

Bryce looked at her worriedly. 'Now, love, don't let one unfortunate experience make you bitter,' he advocated persuasively, patting her arm. 'Not all men are as self-seeking as Jerome, and Lang's suggestion does have considerable merit, you know. Not only from my point of view but from yours as well. A change of scene could be just the thing for you at the moment.'

Nicole retrieved the now golden bread from the toaster and replaced it with more slices. 'New places, new faces?' she quipped laconically.

'You could do worse,' Lang drawled.

'But not much,' she flashed immediately, her chin lifting belligerently. If he didn't stop meddling in her affairs soon she would end up by telling him to his face exactly what she thought of him, guest or not! 'Just because you live there it doesn't make Nullegai the hub of the universe.'

'That's enough, Nicole, there's no call to be rude!' Her father shook his head at her reprovingly. 'Lang's comment was a valid one. You *could* do a lot worse than to come west with me. You know I've been against the idea of you being on your own ever since you first suggested it.'

'And isn't that exactly what I would have to do in Nullegai?' she enquired, not without some slight trace of irony. 'Or is Mr Jamieson proposing that I share your accommodation on his property?'

'No, I think you might find the distance too far to

travel each day, although you would of course always be welcome to share it with him whenever you had any free time,' Lang suggested with a taunting smile.

'Thanks—but no, thanks,' Nicole smiled back, her gaze just as goading. 'My question was meant in a purely theoretical sense, definitely not a practical one.'

'But I'm not so sure it should have been,' her father frowned as he stirred sugar into his tea. 'It sounds an extremely suitable arrangement to me if we could find you decent lodgings in town.'

'There's no hardship there,' put in Lang before she had a chance to divert her parent's train of thought. 'The Misses Guthrie would be only too pleased to have her as a boarder. They've already offered to take in the new schoolteacher who, I'm led to believe, does swimming coaching in his spare time, so the two of them should get along like a house on fire.'

'Except for one thing,' Nicole snapped acidly. '*I* don't happen to be going to Nullegai!'

'Then I won't go either,' Bryce put in heavily, his expression regretful as well as apologetic as he glanced at the younger man. 'When this business of my returning to the bush first came up I only agreed because I believed both you and Cynthia would be married within a short time. Now that you won't be, the conditions unfortunately don't apply any more.'

Nicole's eyes darkened with dismay. She knew how much this job meant to her father, how much he had been looking forward to returning to his chosen profession.

'But you can't give up your job because of *me*,' she gasped. 'It's—it's silly to even think of it, Dad. What if I never marry? Surely you're not planning to still be looking out for me when I've passed thirty or more?'

'We'll face that question if and when it actually happens,' he countered in a repressive tone which had her staring at him helplessly. When he got that particular look about him he was as impossible to move as a mountain.

'But what about Mr Jamieson? You can't let him down like that,' she tried appealing to his personal ethics—strong at the best of times. Not that she cared one way or the other about the inconvenience it might cause Lang Jamieson. In fact, she decided tartly, it might do him good to receive a setback every once in a while. The man was far too damned arrogantly self-assured!

'Yes, well, I feel very badly about that, of course,' he admitted slowly, obviously waging a war with his own conscience. 'But as you know, I've always put my family before anything else, that's why we came to Sydney in the first place. Unless you happen to change your mind there's not much I can do about it, is there?'

A stranger might have called it a subtle form of blackmail, but Nicole knew from past experience that such a thought hadn't entered her father's mind. If she considered it out of the question to move to Nullegai then he would simply do as he had said and refuse to take the post offered, and without a single recrimination—either now or in the future—for the disappointment such an action would create. He enjoyed his daughters' company—as they also did his —and if there was a chance of prolonging their close association he would take it whether it was to the detriment of his career or not. He was just that type of person.

On the heels of these thoughts, however, came others. Until now, hadn't most of the giving been somewhat one-sided in the Lockwood family, and wasn't she really being a little unfair in refusing so stubbornly to even consider the idea? After last night she couldn't honestly say she had a particularly compelling reason for wanting to stay in Sydney, and a complete change probably would be helpful. So just why was she vetoing the suggestion that she accompany her father quite so adamantly?

With a sigh her glance flew from a worried countenance to a bland one and back to the toast she was buttering. Instead of trying to fathom why she was resisting, perhaps she should have asked who! The minute her eyes had clashed with Lang's tawny gaze she felt that inexplicable surge of antagonism which had been present ever since their first disconcerting meeting. There was something too suggestive of a rugged relentlessness about him that she just couldn't bring herself to suffer meekly and which continuously set her on the offensive. The best she could ever possibly hope for in that direction was a stand-off! And in the meantime . . .

'All right, I'll go with you,' she yielded suddenly, albeit still a little grudgingly as she recalled Lang's intervention. 'It's early in the season, so they shouldn't have too much trouble in finding a replacement for me at the pool.'

Bryce reached out a large hand to cover hers momentarily. 'You really mean it, Nicky? You'll come to Nullegai after all?'

'Yes, I'll come,' she replied, arching an eyebrow high as she slanted Lang a gibing look. 'Providing, of course, they do *have* a vacancy for a swimming instructress.'

Her gaze was returned with a slow provoking smile which sent disturbing tremors throughout her nervous system.

'Not any more they don't—it's just been filled,' Lang advised steadily. 'When would you like to start? The same time as your father does with me?'

'Shouldn't I discuss that with the pool manager? That is the usual procedure,' Nicole pointed out in sugared tones.

'Oh, I think we can dispense with the formalities in this instance. If I suggest a commencing date on your behalf I'm sure you'll find him quite happy to accept it.'

Both brows rose in unison this time. 'You have some influence with the pool management, then, do you, Mr Jamieson?'

His expression was one of mock consideration. 'You could say that, I guess,' but without telling her why, 'although I might suggest you make it Lang in future. Not even my employees call me *Mr* Jamieson,' he enlightened her drily.

'You prefer them to use "boss", do you?' innocently.

'If they do it's by their choice, not mine.' Amber eyes narrowed slightly in unspoken warning.

'I see,' she acknowledged, but before she could recklessly add anything further her father was interrupting to ask,

'And these ladies you mentioned, they'll be able to provide lodgings for Nicole, will they?'

'Yes, you can rest easy knowing she'll be well looked after,' Lang reassured him with a smile. 'Ida and Ivy Guthrie are two sixty-year-olds with more energy than most people half their age and who love nothing better than to have a couple of boarders to fuss over. Last year it was two unattached bank tellers, who have since been transferred, but who were fond of declaring that they'd been permanently spoiled for marriage by the ministrations they received.'

'Their idea of the perfect marriage consisting of a well fed stomach and plenty of clean clothes, I presume?' scoffed Nicole.

'I wouldn't know.' Lang fixed her with a gaze of penetrating coolness. 'Although I daresay those qualities would be a sight more appreciated than a caustic tongue!'

It was obvious where that thrust was aimed, but Nicole merely shrugged it off with a sardonic grimace. If he didn't like hearing what she thought about his sex then maybe he shouldn't have been so keen to interfere in her life, because no more would she be the gullible and trusting innocent she had been where men were concerned. She had learnt her lesson and learnt it well. From now on, when the occasion arose, she would be retaliating with whatever weapons she had at hand, and to hell with Lang Jamieson, Jerome Schafer, and the rest of the male half of the population!

CHAPTER TWO

'WHAT was he doing here anyway?' Nicole asked as soon as Lang had left the flat after breakfast. 'Filling in a few hours slumming?'

'No, he was being polite. Something I'm sorry to say you definitely weren't,' her father returned with obvious disappointment. 'As he was in town for the weekend he came out here to meet me and to discuss the work I'll be doing.'

'To make sure for himself that you were competent enough to work on his exalted property, you mean!'

'So? If you owned a place the size and worth of his, would you be prepared to entrust the care of its stock to a man you'd never met, unless you had to?'

Nicole's soft lips twisted wryly. 'No, I guess not,' she owned reluctantly.

'Then how about you stop trying to take out your disillusionment with Jerome on the wrong man, hmm? When all's said and done, Lang Jamieson is my boss and, as such, he's entitled to at least some measure of courtesy from you, love. Your attitude this morning wasn't exactly what I would call helpful.'

'I'm sorry, Dad,' she sighed contritely—for causing him embarrassment, not for being sarcastic towards their guest, 'but what with last night, and then waking up to find it wasn't Cynthia occupying the bed with me, well. . . .'

'Mmm, I wanted to have a few more words with you about that,' he revealed ruefully. 'It came as something of a shock to have my employer telling me he'd just spent the night with my daughter, even though it was accidental.'

'Don't worry, I wasn't really overjoyed about it either!' came the swiftly indignant retort which had him clasping her to him fondly.

'And all because of this damned apartment!' He ran his eyes around the room in dislike. 'I never did take to the place.'

'Well, it was only meant as a temporary arrangement,' Nicole defended it swiftly, her expression saddening as she remembered why, 'and it won't be for much longer now.'

'Still too long for me to want to spend any more time here than I have to. So what do you say to a hasty clearing up, packing our lunch, and then a trip out to French's Forest for a day's trail riding?' he quizzed.

For a second Nicole blinked as tears of recollection involuntarily started into her eyes. It was a far cry from how she had been anticipating spending the day in Jerome's company. Usually at this time of the year their Sundays were spent at the beach, meeting up with friends, lazing on the warm golden sands, surfing, and then finishing off the day with a casual carefree barbecue. Determinedly she shook away the painful memories. That was all behind her now and it was the future which mattered, not the past.

'Sounds okay to me.' She made herself smile up at him and began heading for the kitchen.

It was months since she had last been riding, althoungh her father had always been a regular visitor to the stables, but the more Nicole thought about it as they made ready the more enthusiastic she became. She had always enjoyed the feeling of freedom riding gave her, of being a part *of* nature rather than apart *from* it, as when in a car. And if relaxation wasn't one's objective then it could be stimulating too when powerful legs lengthened stride to make the earth hum beneath flashing hooves and the wind swept one's hair back into a waving banner of shining silk. It seemed just the thing for her today. A heaven-sent opportunity to throw off all her doubts and disappointments for a few hours and to fill her mind with less sombre thoughts instead.

It was a successful ploy and during the following week there wasn't much chance of them returning except for those few times when she actually managed to spare some minutes for herself. The swimming season was getting into full swing with time trials and coaching clinics on behalf of the Swimming Club as well as her normal hours of instruction at the pool, and last-minute alterations to dresses and preparations for Cynthia's wedding the next Saturday.

Fortunately everything went as planned and Cynthia was the epitome of a radiant bride when her proud father escorted her down the aisle of the traditional sandstone church in a cloud of organdie and lace, the bridal bouquets filling the air with a delicate perfume. Later the happy couple were ushered to their car for the start of their honeymoon on the Barrier Reef with much throwing of confetti and rice, together with the usual admonitions and good wishes. The reception continued long after their departure and by the time Nicole and her father finally made it back to the apartment it was to thankfully tumble into bed knowing that the occasion couldn't have been arranged better and that not one single detail had been overlooked.

Although Nicole woudn't have believed it possible, the first few days after the wedding were even more hectic than the ones prior to it had been as they set about tying up any loose ends and making certain they would be ready to leave by Thursday. Not that the journey would take them more than two days of comfortable travelling, but because Bryce had arranged to call at an old friend's property on the way in order to buy a couple of good horses and one or two trained working dogs. In this regard he had, in years past, usually preferred to train his own, but as he had been living in the city for so long now that, of course, hadn't been practical. But he was content. All those years he had spent keeping abreast of new inno-

ACROSS THE GREAT DIVIDE

vations and techniques by reading every rural weekly and farming journal he could lay his hands on had paid off. He was heading back to the country he loved.

As for Nicole, her thoughts weren't nearly so serene and free from anxiety. Tuesday had been an eventful day with an accidental meeting with Jerome while in the city to do some shopping—an encounter made all the more distressing owing to their trite and stilted conversation and their embarrassed desires to be gone from each other's presence—and a telephone call from Lang Jamieson which promptly had her pulse rate increasing the moment she heard his deeply modulated voice informing her that, as he had predicted, the pool committee were extremely pleased to have secured her services and that her accommodation was all arranged with the Guthrie sisters at number ten Wattle Lane. Why he should have affected her in such a breathless manner she couldn't guess—unless it had been brought about by the natural antipathy she felt towards him—but it did give her some long moments of preoccupation on their trip north across the Great Divide.

Nullegai was a thriving little township on the very edge of the western slopes where they levelled out on to the far-reaching plains. The wide tree-lined streets were a mass of colour that Sunday afternoon when Nicole and her father drove down the main street where the purple of bauhinia and the gold of cassia and wattle mingled with the cerise and scarlet of bougainvillaea. There were only a few vehicles angle-parked into the curb and most of those were outside the wide-balconied hotel which stood on a corner between the post office and a general store.

About to stop and ask directions Bryce began slowing, but on Nicole pointing to the opposite side of the intersection and declaring, 'There's Wattle Lane,' as she peered through her sunglasses at the barely discernible name on the faded signpost, he began turning right.

'It's easy to see why it's called Wattle Lane, isn't it?' Nicole grinned as tree upon tree covered in the beautiful yellow blooms stretched before them. Then, some few seconds later, 'It should be the third house on my side. That was number sixteen we just passed.'

Bryce pulled up in front of a large old-fashioned brick house set within well kept grounds where a row of brightly coloured azaleas flowered profusely along the front fence.

'Home sweet home,' he teased gently. 'It's certainly an improvement on what we left behind.'

'You can say that again!' came the dry endorsement. Nicole had been as aware of the utilitarian block of apartments' shortcomings as he had. 'I wonder if the owners are as pleasant as their house and garden?'

He nodded to where a tall grey-haired woman in a

button-through cotton dress was making her way
down the path towards them. 'It shouldn't be long
before we find out. Here comes someone now.'

'Mr Lockwood? Nicole?' The woman beamed at
them amiably as they alighted from the car to greet
her, and after their smiling confirmation, 'Welcome
to Nullegai. I'm Ivy Guthrie. I thought it must have
been you when I saw the float,' as her eyes strayed to
the trailer they were towing with its equine occupants.
'Ida's just putting the kettle on for tea, so do come
along in, I expect you could do with a cup. I always
find it very refreshing myself when ·I've been travelling,' she continued in her non-stop fashion.

Bryce shook his head rapidly. 'Er—not for me,
thanks very much, Miss Guthrie. I'll just carry
Nicky's cases in and then get going again, if you
don't mind?'

'Oh, but you still have a considerable way to go
before you reach Yallambee and I'm sure it would
make it a more enjoyable finish to your drive if you
stayed and had some afternoon tea first,' she proposed earnestly. 'If you're worried about the horses
then by all means drive your wagon into the shade,'
as she waved an arm towards two enormous pine
trees beside the garage, 'and turn them loose in the
paddock at the back of the house for a while. They'll
come to no harm there, it's clean and securely
fenced.'

As his wish to keep moving had been prompted by

his concern for his mounts' welfare Bryce accepted her offer gratefully, and it wasn't long before the two animals were cropping contentedly amidst the knee-high grass, while the two dogs he had purchased scampered out of the station wagon and headed unerringly for the cool darkness beneath the porch.

Inside, the house was a veritable treasure trove of photographs, mementoes, and assorted bric-à-brac. Every piece of available space seemed to have been used to its full advantage. It was, however, spotlessly clean and had clearly been lovingly looked after over the years, for although the furniture and furnishings weren't new or modern in design, they were still in extremely good condition and had an undeniable hallmark of quality stamped on them.

Conversation flowed easily during afternoon tea —with two people as friendly and talkative as Ivy and Ida Guthrie how could it have done otherwise? mused Nicole humorously—and it wasn't long before they were all on a first name footing. Ida, a year younger and an inch or so shorter than her sister, was just as outgoing and only half an hour spent in their spirited company was enough to convince Bryce he had done the right thing in persuading his daughter to come with him. This would be a far more conducive atmosphere for recovering from Jerome's shabby treatment than being alone in a depressing apartment.

Ruefully declining the offer of a third slab of delicious angel cake—Ida apparently didn't believe in anything so minute as a mere slice—Bryce rose to his feet with a muffled sigh.

'Well, love, it looks as if our parting of the ways has finally arrived,' he smiled down at Nicole. 'Unless I start to make a move shortly I won't have time to get settled in before nightfall.'

'But I will be seeing you next weekend?' she queried as they collected her luggage from the station wagon.

'Of course.' He turned towards her in surprise, then grinned broadly. 'That is, unless you find someone else you would rather spend your time with in the meantime.'

'If you're meaning what I think you are, it's highly unlikely. I've sworn off men for life!'

An attitude Bryce had increasingly been aware of over the past two weeks but one he didn't think wise to comment upon at the moment except to enquire jokingly, 'Including me?'

Nicole wrinkled her nose at him in a mixture of exasperation and amusement. 'Not unless you're planning something treacherous too.'

'Not me, love,' he denied with a laugh and a shake of his head as she held open the gauze door because his hands were full. 'As you should know, I'm as open and aboveboard as they come.'

As she brought up the rear as Ivy came out into the hall to show them to the appropriate room, Nicole's

curving lips twisted into a wry smile. Once upon a
time she had believed Jerome was that way as well.

There wasn't much time for Nicole to note a lot
about the bedroom she had been allotted, apart from
the fact that it was wide and high-ceilinged and that
pale pink seemed to be the predominant colour in the
subdued décor, because as soon as her father had de-
posited her cases at the foot of the old fourposter bed
he took his leave of Ivy and Ida and then he was
heading for the paddock. Now that he was on the
move again he was anxious to get back on the road
and complete his journey.

'I'll give you a ring in a couple of days regarding
next weekend,' he said once they had returned the
horses to the float and the dogs to the back of the
wagon. 'Or you should be able to contact me during
the evenings if there are any problems. You've got
the phone number, haven't you?'

'Yes, I've got it,' Nicole confirmed, smiling up at
him as he dropped a kiss on to her smooth forehead
before sliding into the driver's seat and shutting the
door. 'And I'll check out what time I finish at the
pool on Saturdays. We will be spending both days in
town, I take it?' Her brows rose enquiringly.

'Well, that wasn't quite what I had in mind. Having just spent the last fifteen years of my life in town
I think I'll be able to survive without it for a few
weeks,' he countered drily. 'I thought you might like
to come out to the station for a break instead.'

Nicole looped long strands of hair behind her ears and swung her gaze away to stare unseeingly across the gardens. If Yallambee had belonged to someone other than Lang Jamieson she probably wouldn't have hesitated.

'You're not interested in seeing where I live and work?'

The slightly disappointed nuance in her father's tone had her facing him again with a deceptively light laugh. 'Oh, naturally, I am! I was just wondering how I would get there, that's all,' she prevaricated swiftly, her unwillingness being engulfed by her reluctance to hurt his feelings.

'Don't worry, I can always drive in and pick you up.'

'But it's such a long way to come,' she protested.

His eyes took in her worried features affectionately. 'Maybe I just happen to think you're worth it.'

'Flatterer!' she accused with a laugh, but a more natural one this time. 'You should be ashamed of yourself using such blatant methods in order to get your own way.'

'Oh, I am,' he twinkled unrepentantly. 'But now that I've succeeded I'm afraid I really will have to be on my way.' Regretfully he bent forward to switch the V8 engine into powerful life. 'I'll see you on Saturday, Nicky.'

'Okay, Dad.' She leant through the window to kiss his cheek, cautioning, 'Take care,' as he began reversing out of the driveway.

From the gate she gave him one last wave before the vehicle turned out of sight and then walked slowly back to the house, her expression pensive, her thoughts uneasy. She would have preferred to keep well clear of Yallambee Station—and its virile owner —because she strongly doubted her ability to show Lang Jamieson the civility her father expected her to give his employer if their encounters were to be of any but the briefest duration. Why, even now only thinking about him was sufficient to quicken the tempo of her breathing and to send the blood racing more warmly through her veins!

Deliberately, she stopped and expelled a long slow breath, willing her wayward emotions to subside. What she needed was an icy disdain to combat that particular male, not hot-tempered belligerence. Besides, she shrugged bracingly, her father had his own cottage on the property, so it was quite possible that she wouldn't come into contact with Lang at all while she was there. Her lips twitched humorously. And especially if she did her utmost to ensure that was the case.

Suddenly the sound of footsteps on the path behind her intruded upon her meditations and she turned back to see a young man in his middle twenties approaching, his wide mouth curving into a friendly smile.

'Hello there! I guess you must be Nicole Lockwood, Ivy's other boarder. I'm Earl Nicholls,' he introduced himself promptly as they fell into step together.

'I'm pleased to meet you, Earl,' she smiled back at him sincerely. 'And you guessed right, I am Nicole Lockwood. Dad and I arrived about an hour ago.'

Light brown eyebrows, the same colour as his hair, arched questioningly above clear blue eyes. 'He's Lang Jamieson's new stock overseer, isn't he? Ivy and Ida mentioned something about it over breakfast this morning.'

'Mmm, that's right,' she agreed, waiting as he opened the door for her and then stepping into the hallway. 'I'd only just finished waving him goodbye minutes before you came.'

'So now you're all on your own,' he sympathised, but with every evidence of pleasure at his own good fortune. 'If you have nothing else planned you might like to come over to the pool with me. It would be a good opportunity for you to meet Rod Barker, the manager, and that's where I head most afternoons once school's over—I'm a teacher at the school here in town, in case Ivy or Ida didn't tell you.' His head tilted to one side consideringly and he grinned. 'Or are you one of those people who wouldn't be seen dead at their place of employment outside working hours?'

Not surprised that he obviously already knew her occupation, Nicole laughed. 'No, I enjoy swimming too much for that and I thank you for the offer. The only trouble is, I haven't even started my unpacking yet and I really would like to get it done as soon as possible so I have everything straight before starting work tomorrow.'

'You could do it this evening,' persuasively.

She nodded slowly, conceding the point. 'But won't it be too crowded at this time of day for a proper swim?' In Sydney the pool would have been filled with people on such a warm Sunday afternoon.

'Uh-uh!' he wagged a finger at her exultantly. 'You're forgetting how far west you've come. Although our days might be a lot hotter, our nights are still pretty cold during spring, so the water really hasn't had much chance to retain its temperature as yet and only a few very keen souls like myself have been making use of Nullegai's newest community project. In a couple of weeks it will probably be different, but until then it's still possible to work out in the pool without colliding with someone every few feet.'

'In other words ... it's freezing!'

'No, not really,' he grinned at her imaginative grimace. 'Just a little chilly when it first hits you, no more.'

Nicole eyed him suspiciously and then smiled. 'I'll probably regret this, but okay, I'll join you. I never could resist a vacant swimming pool.'

'Good for you.' One blue eye closed in an approving wink. 'I'll meet you at the back door when you're ready, all right?'

'Suits me,' she assented. 'Is the pool very far away?'

'Practically next door. We only have to go through the paddock at the back of the house, cross the road, move a couple of steps to our right and then we'll be facing the entrance.'

'Well, it certainly isn't going to cost me a fortune in fares to and from work, is it?' she laughed.

In her bedroom Nicole unlocked one of the cases and sorted through her many swimsuits, finally deciding on a one piece diagonally striped sunshine yellow and black. Tying her hair back into a ponytail, she thrust a soft rubber cap and a large fringed beach towel into a blue canvas bag and headed for the back door.

'That didn't take long,' Earl commented as he began leading the way out of the garden and into the paddock.

'I always travel light when I'm going swimming,' she explained. 'The operative word being to *swim*, rather than fool around in the water.'

His eyes roamed over her attractive profile somewhat sorrowfully. 'I get the feeling there was a definite message in that statement somewhere.'

It was on the tip of Nicole's tongue to utter a disclaiming, 'I didn't mean it like that!' but she thought better of it and merely gave him a half smile instead as if in regretful endorsement. She wanted no involve-

ments with the opposite sex and it would be better
for both of them if she made that fact perfectly clear
at the outset. He seemed quite nice, but then so had
Jerome!

Leaving the paddock behind they came to the next
wide street where, almost immediately in front of
them, was one of the most elegant residences—it was
far too impressive to be called a house—Nicole had
ever seen. Double-storeyed and Georgian in style, the
sloping ground floor verandah roof supported by
slender fluted columns, it presented a picture of
stately charm amongst tall shady trees and an expanse of close-cropped lawn.

'What a beautiful home!' she exclaimed involuntarily, stopping and staring at it more closely. 'Who
does it belong to?'

'Eunice Blanchard—or *Mrs* Blanchard to the likes
of you and me,' Earl supplied in the driest of tones.
'She's very much a member of the local social set and
only those she considers her peers are permitted the
use of a more familiar form of address. I've only met
her once—her son's in my class at school—but that
was enough.' His lips curled sardonically. 'A little of
her type goes an awful long way where I'm concerned.'

One last look at the lovely building and Nicole resumed walking. 'Maybe she improves on further
acquaintance,' she suggested cheerfully. 'A lot of
people do.'

Earl shrugged doubtfully. 'You'll probably be able to gauge the truth of that for yourself very shortly. From what I've heard, she's planning to enrol Gervaise in the Swimming Club as soon as she can.'

'Gervaise is her son?'

'Mmm, that's him, but for heaven's sake, don't fall into the trap of calling him Gerry, or you'll have Mama down on top of you like a ton of bricks!'

'The reason for your single meeting?' she surmised with a grin.

'And how!' His blue eyes rolled expressively. 'You would have thought I'd committed the worst crime in the book.'

'I *had* better watch myself then, hadn't I?' she laughed. 'Thanks for the warning.'

Before changing into her costume Nicole spent the first three-quarters of an hour being shown over the complex by Rod Barker, the man the local Council had persuaded to leave a similar position down south in order to manage it for them. Somewhat short of stature but friendly of disposition, they soon found themselves discussing with congenial affinity the pros and cons of the various pool management schemes and coaching mechanics they had each been exposed to from time to time.

As Rod's fourteen year old daughter, Marilyn, was the only other person training that afternoon their conversation was undisturbed and they were completely unaware of the passing time until Earl emerged from the water to remind Nicole with a grin, 'Hey! I brought you over here for a *swim*, remember?'

On looking up to see the time displayed by the clock mounted on the wall above the kiosk, Nicole clapped a hand to her mouth in amazement.

'I'm sorry, Earl, I'll be right with you,' she apologised promptly. And to Rod, 'You said my first lesson was for ten in the morning?'

'That's right,' he nodded his agreement. 'Pat Wheeler's two little girls. I think you'll find they'll take to it quite well, because you couldn't find a couple of kids more anxious to get started.'

After hurriedly making use of the dressing rooms Nicole was still pushing her hair under her cap when she rejoined Earl at the poolside.

'It's my own fault, but I bet it's even colder now than it was,' she pulled a rueful face on noting the darkening shadows of the nearby trees creeping further and further across the rippling water. 'I shouldn't have stayed talking so long.'

The minute she dived in Nicole knew she had been correct in her prediction—it *was* cold!—but as she unwaveringly followed one of the lines marked on the bottom of the pool down its fifty-metre length in a deliberately paced free-style the temperature of the water became less noticeable, as always, and by the time she had concluded her sixth lap it felt no different than it did in the middle of summer.

Earl had accompanied her on the first three laps, but after that he had been content to just watch and now he drifted towards her with a respectful look on his face.

'Not only pretty to look at, but pretty to watch as well,' he acknowledged her proficiency with patent admiration. 'You sure don't waste any energy, do you?'

'I hope not,' she chuckled. 'After all, that's what swimming is all about. Channelling every ounce of effort towards that single goal—propulsion! Not that it's strictly necessary for an instructor to be able to swim well, of course. The best swimmers don't always make the best coaches.'

'Present company excluded, I trust?' he proposed with a twinkle.

'Oh, yes, that goes without saying,' Nicole declared in the same light vein, remembering Lang's comment that Earl liked to coach in his spare time too. 'But now,' she couldn't help a spontaneous shiver, 'I suggest we start moving again or Nullegai could very well find itself deprived of our invaluable services— due to the contraction of pneumonia—before we get an opportunity to display even a portion of our combined talents. How does a few more laps appeal to you?'

'Okay by me. Free-style again?' he asked.

She shook her head and laughed. 'No, let's make it butterfly. We'll warm up faster.'

In the end, by mutual consent, they progressed into a medley, with neither one of them making a bid to outpace the other but taking their time and concentrating on their strokes.

'That was good,' reflected Nicole pleasurably as they headed homewards later. 'It's always such a treat to be able to swim uninterrupted.'

'Mmm, now you know why I'm making the most of it while I can,' Earl returned wryly. 'It won't last for much longer, unfortunately.'

'No, I suppose not,' she smiled, then went on to ask thoughtfully, 'But just how many of the children in Nullegai are able to swim? Would you have any idea?'

He hunched his shoulders in a brief gesture of ignorance. 'Not the actual numbers, no, but from what was said at the Club meeting last week I gather that at least some of them have made the hundred-and-twenty-mile trip to Franklyn for the Government's annual Learn to Swim campaigns during the holidays. As for the rest,' he shrugged again, 'I'd take a guess and say they've made good use of the local river and creeks for their initiation into the sport. No doubt your father's boss would be able to give you more information in that regard. Don't forget I've only been here a fortnight myself.'

Nicole's forehead creased sharply. She had forgotten, although that wasn't the reason for her frown.

'And what makes Lang Jamieson the expert?' she

demanded, not a little sarcastically. 'He may be big-time in the area,' that much had become evident during afternoon tea with the Guthrie sisters, 'but surely that doesn't entitle him to the position of Big Brother too!'

If he was taken aback by her unexpected vehemence, Earl didn't show it, merely laughing and explaining, 'No, but as the duly elected President of the new Swimming Club, as well as being one of the driving forces behind the pool project, it's only natural that he has a better knowledge concerning these matters than most other people in town.'

'He's the President of the Swimming Club!' Nicole repeated, astonished. That was something he had conveniently omitted to tell her.

Earl peered at her closely. 'Didn't you know? I'd have thought that would have come out when he interviewed you.'

Interviewed her! Hah! Railroaded her into taking the job, more like! He had known full well that if he had allowed that little piece of information to slip out nothing would have persuaded her to come to Nullegai. It was quite bad enough him being her father's employer, without her having to work in close conjunction with him too!

Aloud she dismissed it with as much indifference as she could manage. 'No, he didn't mention it. In fact, he didn't say much about the Swimming Club at all.'

And now she knew why!

CHAPTER THREE

As the days continued hot and sunny and the water temperature rose accordingly, Nicole became a familiar figure to an increasing number of people as she paced alongside the pool advising the more advanced of her charges, or else joined some of the younger and less competent ones in the water in order to demonstrate and to build their confidence.

Apparently a lot of parents had only been waiting for the arrival of a permanent instructor before enrolling their children for lessons and now that the word was spreading she soon found her services to be in almost constant demand. So much so on some days that it wasn't until Rod was closing up for the night that she could manage to get in a few practice laps herself.

Earl still came every day after school, but as that was one of Nicole's busiest times he usually had to be content with swimming alone, or hurried snatches of conversation in between instructions to the classes he helped her with. Not that Nicole regretted her preoccupation—actually she was rather grateful—because it prevented him from monopolising any more of her time than he did already. He was likeable

enough, and perhaps it was only to be expected that
since they were both newcomers to the town they
should become friendly, but his continuous efforts
to accompany her wherever she went—even when it
was only a short walk to the mailbox after tea to post
a letter to her sister—were becoming a little too per-
sistent. Consequently, it had been a relief to be able
to tell him, after her father had telephoned as arranged, that she couldn't attend the party one of his
fellow teachers was giving that Saturday because she
would be going out to Yallambee for the weekend as
soon as the early morning training session was concluded.

She could, she supposed, have told him outright
that she really wasn't interested in furthering their
acquaintanceship—clearly that negative smile she
had given him during their first meeting hadn't been
sufficient of a deterrent—but as they also boarded at
the same address she considered it could put some
strain upon the normally happy atmosphere and decided against it. Anyway, as the season progressed,
more and more of her time would be taken up at the
pool and his opportunities to claim her attention
would decrease proportionately.

Nicole arrived at the pool before Rod on Saturday
morning and was greeted by an eager squad of her
regular pupils as she unlocked the gates, their happy
chattering fading as they swiftly made for the changing rooms.

'Shall I get the kickboards out of the equipment room, Miss Lockwood?' asked the last girl as she came through.

In the middle of ticking off the appropriate numbers on the attendance sheet, Nicole smiled an agreeing, 'Yes, thank you, Rhonda,' and selecting the correct key on the ring she had just returned to her pocket handed it across to the diminutive pigtailed blonde together with the advice, 'I thought we would begin with all of you doing a couple of laps of freestyle kicking today. You can tell the others that when they're ready to start, if you like.'

'Yes, Miss Lockwood,' came the almost sighed acknowledgment as pride at being the bearer of such important information split her features with a beaming grin.

It could only have been seconds before Rhonda was back again to return the keys and then she was hurrying across the grass to where the rest of the class had congregated at the pool's edge, her steps punctuated every so often with an ecstatic skip which had Nicole's lips curving softly. That was one of Rhonda's most endearing qualities and what made her such a rewarding child to teach. She approached everything with such boundless enthusiasm. No matter what was asked of her she put all she possessed into achieving the desired result and, in consequence, was progressing faster than Nicole would have believed possible.

'Excuse me. . . .'

A young voice suddenly broke in up on Nicole's musings and she turned to discover a rather sharp-featured boy of some eleven years eyeing her unblinkingly from the other side of the pay window. His expensively tailored and monogrammed track suit immediately set him apart from the other children she had met so far, as did that unwavering grey-green gaze which was disconcertingly aloof in one so young.

'I'm Gervaise Blanchard,' he continued in a tone which hinted at self-importance now that he had her attention. 'My mother sent me down for private lessons in stroke correction.'

Blanchard? For a moment a slight furrow appeared between Nicole's winged brows, then just as rapidly disappeared. Now she remembered. His mother owned the beautiful mansion further along the street.

'I'm sorry, Gervaise, but I don't give private lessons on Saturday,' she smiled apologetically. 'However you're welcome to join the rest of my class, if you'd care to. We'll be concentrating on technique this morning anyway.'

When he didn't reply she was prompted to ask, 'You probably know most of the children here, don't you?' thinking perhaps the remoteness he exuded was only a cover for shyness.

His eyes flickered briefly as he looked towards the

group, girls and boys, who were preparing to take to the water.

'Yes, I know them,' he admitted with a dispassionate hunching of one shoulder. 'But I'm supposed to have private lessons. My mother says you only get the best if you pay the most for it.'

'Yes, well, that may be true sometimes, but definitely not always,' Nicole argued gently against what she considered to be a somewhat biased theory. 'I try to give everyone whatever amount of tuition and guidance they need, whether it's singly or collectively.'

'But my mother said. . . .'

Nicole gave a defeated laugh and held up one hand in surrender. His parent had obviously convinced him of the doubtful superiority of private lessons.

'Okay, if that's what you want. How about Monday after school, does that suit you?'

Instead of answering he had a question of his own to ask. 'Why can't it be this afternoon, or tomorrow?'

'Because once this session is concluded,' she gestured towards the children already in the water, 'I won't be working any more this weekend.'

'But you could make an exception in *my* case, couldn't you?'

His return was made with such a haughty conviction of his own importance that Nicole almost gasped her surprise out loud.

'No, I'm sorry, Gervaise, but I couldn't,' she replied firmly, then feeling she might have been a little too abrupt went on to explain, 'You see, I won't even be in Nullegai. I'm spending the next two days with my father at Yallambee.'

'Oh, yes, he's Lang Jamieson's new hired hand, isn't he?'

'That's one way of putting it,' she agreed drily, curbing a mounting desire to box his ears for the deliberate denigration in his tone.

'Do *you* know Lang?' He surveyed her interestedly.

'I've met him once, that's all,' she shrugged. It wasn't a subject she cared to pursue and certainly not with this particular eleven-year-old. 'But now you'll have to excuse me, I'm afraid. I have to get on with my class.' As she turned to leave she looked back at him questioningly. 'Shall I mark you down for Monday, then, or not?'

With an exaggerated sigh Gervaise nodded. 'I suppose so ... although I don't expect my mother will be very pleased. She wanted me to start today.'

Nicole wryly suspected that type of comment had been used on previous occasions to bring about marked changes in attitude, but this time it fell on deaf ears because she only sent him a faintly apologetic look before continuing on her way. If Eunice Blanchard didn't like the arrangement she could find someone else to coach her son. From what Nicole had seen of Gervaise so far she wasn't overly impressed!

The lesson went well that morning with most of the children showing a definite improvement in their style and the rest advancing only a little less noticeably. Rhonda was, once again, the star of the team and as always she was also the last to leave the pool.

'I saw you talking to Gervaise Blanchard earlier. Is he going to join our squad, Miss Lockwood?' she asked as they returned the equipment to its appropriate shelf.

Nicole made a slight negative movement with her head. 'No, his mother wants him to have private tuition, so he's coming on Monday after school.'

'That's good.'

'What makes you say that? Don't you like him?'

'Not much,' was Rhonda's candid reply, followed by a wide grin as she relayed, 'We can hardly wait until next year when he goes to boarding school!'

Tempted though she was to probe a little further for the reasons causing her dislike, Nicole held her tongue. Her small companion, however, wasn't nearly so reticent.

'He always acts as if he's so much better than the rest of us,' Rhonda explained with an expressive grimace. 'He doesn't deserve to have that nice Mr Jamieson as his father.'

Alarm bells set up a ringing inside Nicole's head. '*Lang* Jamieson?' she quizzed, and after receiving a corroborating nod, gasped, 'Is Gervaise's father?'

Rhonda covered her face with her hands and began giggling uncontrollably. 'Oh, no, he's just going to marry Mrs Blanchard. He'll be Gervaise's new daddy. You know, a—a. . . .'

'Stepfather?' supplied Nicole helpfully.

'That's it,' Rhonda nodded equably, then amended it with a qualifying, 'Or that's what Gervaise reckons. Of course he could be telling fibs, he sometimes does.'

'About something so important?'

Thin shoulders lifted uncertainly. 'He might,' was as far as Rhonda was prepared to commit herself, and Nicole didn't press her. Her remarks had been quite enlightening as it was without asking for more.

In fact, Nicole was still pondering over them after she had bidden Rhonda and Rod goodbye and was walking slowly home. Not that there was any reason why her thoughts should have lingered on the prospect of her father's employer marrying the renowned Mrs Blanchard, but linger they did, and it wasn't until she had reached the house and began talking to Ivy that she was able to put them out of her head.

'Dad hasn't been yet?' was her immediate question after checking to see whether the familiar station wagon was parked out the front.

'No, dear, not yet,' Ivy reported with a smile, her arms full of sheets she was in the process of taking out to the laundry. 'But I expect he'll be along before you've changed and finished your packing. Don't forget to let me have your track suit so I can have it cleaned and ready for you on Monday, will you

Nicky?' she added over her shoulder as she continued
on her way.

'No, I won't, thanks, Ivy,' Nicole called back, and
entered her room.

Quickly she stripped off the red and white suit, as
well as the plain red costume she had been wearing
underneath it, and changed into a slim-fitting tunic
of orange and black cotton with a wide square neck-
line which displayed an expanse of smooth tanned
skin to advantage. A light addition of lipstick to the
soft contours of her mouth was the only make-up she
used, and after giving her hair a thorough brushing
she slipped a bandeau into position and swept the
long silken strands over her shoulders. A few more
oddments were tossed into the small case she was
taking with her, the locks fastened, then she hurried
down the hallway with those of her clothes which
needed washing.

On her way back from the laundry Nicole heard
the sound of a man's voice coming from the kitchen
where Ida was doing her weekend baking and, think-
her father must have arrived without her being aware
of it, she pushed open the door and walked into the
room with her eyes sparkling expectantly.

Only it wasn't her parent's stocky frame which was
leaning back so casually against the waist-high cupboards, it was a much taller though no less muscular
one, and they weren't deep brown eyes that swung to

focus on her expressive face, they were gleaming golden-hazel.

'Oh!'

The exclamation tumbled from her lips in sheer surprise at finding herself so precipitately in Lang's presence—she had anticipated having some time in which to prepare herself before that eventuality occurred—and it was only after some seconds had elapsed that she could recover her scattered thoughts sufficiently to bid him, 'Good morning,' and even then it was in a faintly flustered tone which showed all too plainly for her liking just how restive she was in his company.

She tried to explain away her uneasiness with a shrugged, 'I thought you must have been Dad when I heard another voice in here. I'm expecting him to call for me at any minute.'

'Sorry, kitten, he was unavoidably detained,' Lang smiled across at her with an expression of sympathy she was positive was only feigned. 'But as I'd already made arrangements to drive in this morning myself, I said I would drop by and collect you.'

'That was kind of you,' she conceded, but with irony uppermost. He made it sound as if she was a piece of lost luggage. 'And just what was it that *unavoidably* detained him?' An upward slanting brow placed even more emphasis on the word.

'A rather valuable cow,' he divulged, his lips crooking appreciatively. 'She's apparently decided this morning is as good a time as any to have difficulty in calving.'

While as stock overseer it was, of course, her father's responsibility to be there.

'Oh,' she murmured again, quietly, and shifted her weight from one foot to the other. 'Well, I—I'm ready when you are. That is, if you've concluded your business.' The sooner they started the trip the quicker it would be over.

'It's finished.' Lang inclined his head sharply and the scrape of steel in his voice had Nicole searching his face speculatively.

Taking a swift guess, she surmised that whatever business had brought him to town had been pungently conducted. Unless she was very much mistaken, someone, somewhere in Nullegai, was feeling rather sorry for themselves right at the moment.

'Where's your case?' he asked Nicole, his voice resuming its customary intonation.

She waved a hand towards the hall. 'Down there.'

'You're sure you won't have a cup of tea before you leave?' Ida turned from taking a tray of crisp almond biscuits from the oven to glance at each of them in turn.

A smiling shake of her head was Nicole's agreement with Lang's, 'No, thanks, Ida,' which he followed with an extenuating, 'I'd rather not be away any longer than I have to.'

'Ah, yes, the little mother-to-be.' Her lips pursed

thoughtfully. 'It must have been something very important to have brought you to town at all.'

'It was,' Lang agreed, wryly recognising her seemingly innocent remark for what it was—an interested probing for additional information. 'But now. . . .'

As he clearly wasn't about to satisfy her curiosity Ida gave in gracefully, wishing them a safe journey as she accompanied them through the house and waving them goodbye from the front porch as they drove away in the dark green Falcon.

'Well, what do you think of our Guthrie sisters?' Lang spared Nicole a fleeting look as they turned out of Wattle Lane and on to the main highway. 'They're quite a pair, aren't they?'

'Very much so,' she smiled, and deeming it a safe topic to follow, asked, 'Have you known them long?'

'All my life. Their father used to own the property next to ours and they only moved into town about five years ago after he died.'

'And neither of them has ever married?'

Lang shook his head slowly. 'No, it seems the Second World War took care of that. Ivy lost her fiancé in North Africa and Ida's never returned from New Guinea.'

'How dreadful!' Nicole frowned in commiseration. 'Yet, talking to them, you would never guess they'd experienced such tragedies in their lives.'

'It was a long time ago and, as I told you in Sydney, the pain lessens with time.' A sidelong glance of glittering amber temporarily held her captive. 'A few more months and you probably won't even be able to remember what—Jerome, wasn't it?—looked like.'

His intrusion into her personal life brought Nicole's chin fractionally higher. 'And that's where you couldn't be more wrong,' she informed him coolly. 'I fully intend to remember every single detail about him. Just so I'm not tempted to make the same mistake again, you understand.'

'One deflating episode and you want to cry quits, is that it?' he retorted promptly on a slightly jeering note. 'Well, well, who would have thought it, little Miss Lockwood is fainthearted!'

'I am not!' Nicole half turned in her seat to flare at him hotly. 'I simply refuse to be taken in again by a lot of sweet nothings. Having once removed the rose-coloured glasses I was viewing the world through, I can assure you I'm not about to put them back on again.'

'No, don't you,' he commended sardonically. 'That would be too much like admitting you might have made an error in condemning every male because of the actions of one man. Only I wouldn't advise you to make your jaundiced views known too widely ... someone might feel inclined to take up the challenge.'

'What challenge?'

His lips tilted into a mocking smile. 'The one you're throwing out so recklessly,' he drawled. 'In case you haven't realised it, those sentiments of yours are a flagrant invitation for some male to decide he's going to be the one to change your mind.'

Nicole sniffed disdainfully. 'He'd be a fool to try.'

'Because he'd be wasting his time?'

Lazy eyes slid over her with such a provocative glint that she flushed fierily. Suddenly she could recall the reassuring feel of those strong competent hands holding her close to that wide chest, the texture of his bronzed skin against her cheek, and she shook her head angrily to dislodge the memory.

'His time and mine,' she snapped.

'So how does Nicholls feel about that?'

'Earl?' she questioned in amazement. 'How should I know?'

'You mean, he hasn't been your constant companion for the last week?'

Living out of town hadn't seemed to affect his knowledge of what went on in Nullegai.

'If he has it was by his choice, certainly not by my invitation!'

'But he does have his uses, I gather,' his voice flicked at her scornfully. 'Like being a convenient bulwark for you to hide behind.'

'Oh, don't be so ridiculous!' she stormed, resentful of his reasoning. 'Why should I need anyone to hide behind? I said I wasn't *interested* in your sex, not that I was *afraid* of them!'

'Just afraid of the consequences of becoming involved, is that it?'

Pressing her lips together tightly, Nicole turned away again to stare at the scenery speeding past. The endless paddocks filled with maturing crops of wheat, oats and barley. Smooth-coated cattle and thickly woolled sheep foraging amid grass made lush by the spring rains. And the black strip of bitumen they were travelling on which stretched inexorably towards the shimmering horizon. In some respects the road reminded Nicole of her companion. They were both undeviating, unmovable, and completely unyielding!

She swung back to face him with a gibe on her lips. 'Even if it was, I still don't see what concern it would be of yours! Or can't your masculine pride accept the fact that it's possible for a woman to remain unaffected by male advances?'

Lang's ensuing smile was a slow one, and so unexpected that it set Nicole's heart pounding against her ribs before she could attempt to control it.

'That would all depend upon which male was doing the advancing, wouldn't it?' he taunted.

Nicole swallowed hard and dropped her gaze to her clenching fingers. In one short moment it had been frighteningly demonstrated just how tenuous her defences really were. It was only her prior knowledge that his attention had already been focused in another direction that enabled her to reply with any show of conviction.

'Not if one remembers that you're all tarred with

the same brush! After all, we both know there isn't one of you who's above withholding pertinent facts if it suits your purposes, don't we?' she denounced belligerently.

Although it was obvious he knew exactly which omission on his part she was referring to, Lang didn't seem at all put out by her accusation. In fact, he appeared more amused than abashed—much to Nicole's annoyance.

'It never occurred to me you would attach so much importance to a mere name,' he laughed.

'Oh, not just any name, Lang, but yours!—as President of the Swimming Club. You knew damned well I wouldn't have taken the job if I'd known that!'

One dark brow quirked in mocking disbelief. 'All because you took exception to the manner of our meeting?'

Rosy colour stained Nicole's cheeks and she rushed into indignant speech. 'I did *not* take exception to the manner of our meeting,' she denied vehemently, but at the baiting look which entered his gold-flecked eyes, corrected herself embarrassedly, 'Well, of course, I did, but—but that wasn't the reason.'

'Then why don't you tell me what was?' he invited smoothly.

'It—it's obvious, isn't it?' she stammered, a dark abyss abruptly looming in her mind where her reasons should have been.

What could she say? That she resented him for

knowing of Jerome's defection? That she believed he had ruthlessly used that defection to his own advantage because they needed an instructor at the Nullegai pool? Or that he had the perturbing ability to make her disastrously aware of his physical attraction?

Eventually she made do with, 'The President of the Club and the coach are the two who have to work closest together, and we—we're just not in accord. All we can manage is to antagonise one another.'

Lang pulled out to overtake a cattle truck in front of them and then swung back into the appropriate lane again.

'So what are you suggesting? That one of us resigns because you can't keep your personal and business feelings separate?'

His implication that any confrontation was only likely to be caused by her had Nicole's temper rising. 'I wasn't suggesting anything!' she retaliated tartly. 'I was merely pointing out that, had you seen fit to tell the truth in the first place, neither of us would now be in the position where we're forced into each other's company when we would both rather avoid it!'

'And if you hadn't decided to blame every male for one man's actions it wouldn't have mattered one iota whether I'd told you or not,' he bit out coldly in return. 'The only reason you're so uptight in my company is because you know damned well I'm not going to pamper that punctured ego of yours!'

'That's not true!' she denied furiously, her eyes shining with a militant light. 'You're the last person in the world I would want, or expect, any compassion from.'

'I'm pleased to hear it,' he applauded sarcastically. 'And a golden opportunity for you to prove it presents itself in our being able to work harmoniously together for the Club, doesn't it?'

Right at that moment Nicole would have agreed to walk barefoot over live coals in her efforts to disabuse Lang of the idea that she wanted sympathy from him.

'How right you are,' she endorsed swiftly, eagerly. 'It will be a pleasure to show you just how far removed from reality your theory really is.' And show him she would, even if it took the last ounce of self-control she possessed!

For a time there was silence in the car and as the miles slipped past Nicole concentrated her attention upon the view outside. It brought back the few almost forgotten memories she had to her early childhood before they had moved to the city. Carefree years when Cynthia and herself had so often gone fishing for yabbies—or freshwater crayfish, as some people called them—in the creek which ran through the property where their father had worked, and had come home to a scolding for having managed to get themselves so wet and muddy. Not that the countryside was similar—they had lived closer to the coast

with its rocky escarpment and denser vegetation—
but the scents that the breeze was wafting into the
vehicle were familiar and they irresistibly stirred
deep chords of remembrance within her subcon-
scious.

Presently they branched off the highway on to a
secondary road where flocks of crested pigeons took
to the air at their approach, but the sharp-eyed and
powerful-beaked kookaburras remained motionless
on their fence posts as they watched for the slightest
movement that would indicate the presence of a
quarry. They were fearless birds who adapted easily
to backyard feeding and whose snake-killing abilities
were well known, and appreciated, by many.

On either side of them broadacre paddocks predicted a bumper harvest and as she surveyed the nod-
ding ears of still faintly green wheat Nicole was
tempted to remark humorously, 'That's a tremendous
amount of cakes and pastries out there,' in an attempt
to lighten the somewhat strained atmosphere which
existed inside the car before they reached Yallambee.

Because of the lack of traffic on the road Lang's
glance rested on her honey-toned features longer than
it would otherwise have done.

'It had better not be,' he countered drily.

'Oh?' Nicole's expression mirrored her surprise
and wariness. 'Why not?'

He sent her a lazy look that came perilously close
to demolishing her nervous system. 'Because those

foods are made from low protein, soft wheat, and this is prime hard, high protein country. Wheat isn't just wheat, you know,' he told her with a touch of drawling mockery. 'There are different classifications, different regions that suit each one best.'

'Would this be used for bread, then?' she asked, and waved a hand to indicate the rows they were passing, determined to learn what she could even if it did mean having to suffer more of those rather amused corrections.

Lang nodded equably this time. 'High-quality breads, as well as products like noodles and semolina. Loaf bread is manufactured from what's known as just hard wheat, not prime hard.'

'Which, in turn, is followed by the soft you mentioned?'

'Uh-uh! In between comes standard white, which makes a general all-purpose flour.'

Well, well, as he had said, wheat really wasn't just wheat after all, Nicole acceded inwardly. Perhaps she should have paid more attention to those rural periodicals her father had read over the years, then she wouldn't have needed to put her ignorance on display for Lang's gratification at all.

With a sigh she settled back in her seat and gave him a sideways glance. 'Is it much farther?' she asked.

'Not very,' he replied, and pointed to their right. 'This is part of Yallambee we're passing now.'

On the verge of showing her curiosity, Nicole clamped down on her automatic response to look about her with interest and merely nodded instead. She wouldn't give him the satisfaction of knowing how inquisitive she was regarding the property whose name had cropped up in so many conversations she had had in Nullegai. All the same, she couldn't quite forbid herself a covert inspection from beneath long curling lashes and was grudingly impressed.

She didn't know where the boundaries were, of course, but as her father had been employed as stock overseer, and as there wasn't an animal of any kind in sight, she presumed there was far more to the station than could be seen from the car. Disappointingly, there had been no sign of a house in her hasty scrutiny and she was forced to contain her increasing interest on this aspect until another twenty minutes had elapsed.

When the building finally came into view after they had traversed a eucalypt-shaded bridge spanning a bubbling creek of crystal clearness, Nicole privately considered the waiting had been worthwhile. Surrounded by glossy-leaved kurrajongs and slender belahs, and set amid gardens of eye-catching design and colour, it was a magnificent two-storeyed structure which reflected a Mediterranean rather than colonial architecture with white arches forming an arcade beneath the columns and railings of the upper balcony.

Instead of following the curving driveway to the front of his home, Lang continued on past the gardens towards a neat timber-framed cottage standing within its own white-fenced area of ground some distance away. But as Yallambee homestead disappeared from sight behind veiling trees and shrubs Nicole couldn't help making the rather awed exclamation,

'Surely you don't live there all on your own!' She just couldn't imagine such a huge residence being occupied by only one person.

'Not entirely,' Lang owned a trifle ruefully. 'My housekeeper and her husband have an apartment at the rear of the house, some of the unmarried staff have their meals there even though they have their own sleeping quarters, and I also have a large tribe of brothers and sisters who periodically descend upon the place together with their numerous offspring.'

There was a suggestion of censure in Nicole's gaze. 'You sound as if you don't like children,' she reproved.

'Oh, I like them well enough ... when under control,' he retorted wryly as he brought the vehicle to a halt outside the cottage. 'But I happen to come from a family of nine children, the rest of whom seem bent on breaking my mother's record of three sets of twins. At the moment, I believe the count of my various nieces and nephews stands in the vicinity of seventeen —all under the age of ten, I might add—and when they arrive en masse pandemonium really isn't quite adequate to describe the result.' His eyes narrowed slightly and the beginnings of a taunting smile appeared at the corners of his mouth. 'You just wait until Christmas and you'll be able to judge for yourself.'

'No, thanks,' Nicole declined with a grin. As she was involved with children just about every day she didn't have to stretch her imagination too far to picture how it would be with so many youngsters just out to amuse themselves! Then, as Lang came around to open the door for her and she alighted, 'You weren't a twin, though, were you?' Her head tipped sideways in consideration.

Lang's demeanour suddenly became less relaxed. 'What makes you say that?' he probed.

'Only the thought that I really couldn't see you as being anything but a one-off,' she smiled banteringly and, before he had a chance to reply, began hurrying to meet her father who had appeared in the cottage doorway.

She might have been manoeuvred into agreeing to a conciliatory relationship for the sake of the Swimming Club, but he could think again if he thought that meant she was going to be as amenable on a personal level too. Her attitude might have had to change, but her feelings certainly hadn't!

CHAPTER FOUR

'HELLO, love,' Bryce greeted his daughter with a hug and a kiss. 'Sorry I couldn't get into town to pick you up, but animals aren't always prepared to fit in with our timetables, I'm sorry to say. Did Lang explain?'

'Mmm, he said a cow was in difficulty calving,' she recounted briefly, and gave him a questioning look. 'How is she now, Dad? Okay?'

'Right as rain,' he smiled in patent relief. 'It was touch and go for a while, but we managed to turn the little devil the right way in the end and now she has a fine-looking calf at foot.' His gaze went past her to Lang's tall figure as he strode towards them carrying Nicole's luggage. 'You'll be pleased to hear that Sable was delivered of a bull calf about an hour after you left,' he repeated for his employer's benefit.

Not surprisingly, Lang was obviously pleased. 'Thanks, Bryce, you did a good job. I'm only sorry I had to leave you with it as I know from personal experience that it's not as easy as you're making it sound,' he observed knowledgeably. 'Once I've put this inside,' indicating the case he was holding, 'I'll go down and take a look at them both.'

'I'll go with you,' Bryce offered casually as they

started for the cottage. And to Nicole, 'How about you, Nicky? Do you want to see him too?'

The chance to escape from Lang's forceful presence was too good to miss and she shook her head with a passable look of regret.

'Perhaps later,' she suggested. 'I'd like to settle in and have a drink first, if that's all right with you?'

'Anything you like,' he accepted her decision amiably, standing back to allow her to enter the house first and relieving Lang of her suitcase which he left in the hall when they moved into the sitting room. 'I shouldn't be long.'

'There's no rush. I can always start preparing lunch if you're not back by the time I've finished having a good look round,' she smiled.

Lang began moving back towards the door, apparently no more desirous of continuing their meeting than Nicole was.

'We'll see you later, then.' His head dipped towards her summarily.

'I expect so,' she nodded just as briefly. 'And—and thank you for the lift.'

'No trouble, it didn't take me out of my way.'

Which remark left Nicole with the distinct feeling that had it done so his offer to her father would never have been made. No doubt as far as he was concerned, she could have stayed in Nullegai until Bryce was free to drive in for her himself.

As soon as they had left Nicole transferred the few

clothes she had brought with her to the wardrobe and dressing table in the small but adequate bedroom she was to occupy for the night and then proceeded to explore the rest of the house as she made her way to the kitchen in order to find something cold to drink

Not bad, she conceded dispassionately, at the completion of her tour as she poured herself a glass of lemonade from a bottle in the fridge. It was clean and tidy and quite big enough for her father's requirements. Actually, she liked the kitchen best of all. It was a bright cheery room painted in lemon and white, with plenty of cupboards, modern equipment, and wide windows above the stainless steel sink which presented a panoramic view across the property for whoever was doing the washing up.

However, after a frowning check of the pantry, what wasn't nearly so heartening was the fact that the store of tinned foods she had purchased for her father was still standing on the shelves, hardly depleted, and the fresh vegetables she had made him promise to purchase on his way out of Nullegai the weekend before still lay in the fridge, presumably untouched.

It was a possibility that hadn't occurred to Nicole previously and her forehead now creased with worry. Naturally, when they had all lived together either Cynthia or herself had done most of the cooking, and the thought that her father might not be bothering to eat properly now that he had to care for himself was decidedly disturbing.

Luckily, though, some of the vegetables had kept well enough in their cold environment and she immediately set about rectifying her father's omission by making him as appetising a meal as possible with those that were still edible and supplementing them with a few of the tins in the cupboard. The bread she found in a large container in the pantry felt surprisingly new and she guessed it was home-baked—probably by Lang's housekeeper—and she was in the middle of cutting a pile of crusty slices when Bryce returned.

'My, you've been busy,' he commented as he entered the room and saw the laden table. 'Were you expecting Lang to stay for lunch?'

Nicole's eyes widened in protest. 'No!' she denied strongly. 'It's for you. From the amount of food you've still got in the cupboard and the fridge you must have been on a starvation diet all week!'

'Diet?' Momentarily his face was a study in bewilderment, and then he started to laugh. 'No, I've been having my meals up at Government House,' an outstretched arm motioned towards the homestead, 'that's why very little has been touched round here.'

'Oh, I see.' Nicole sighed in relief at his explanation, although another emotion was soon taking over and she promptly went on to scoff, 'Government House? Don't you think that's overdoing things just a little too much? I know Lang Jamieson is the biggest frog in the pond round these parts,' just how big she hadn't realised until she saw Yallambee, 'but when all's said and done, he is still only your employer ... not some omnipotent warlord from the Middle Ages!'

'And you're clearly still taking out your disappointment in Jerome's behaviour on the wrong person!' Bryce rebuked sharply—in a sharper tone of voice than Nicole could ever remember him using before, in fact. 'The expression is an old one in the bush and commonly used to signify the main homestead. It certainly isn't unique to this particular property and if I choose to describe it as such it's by my decision, not at someone else's suggestion, as you appear to be inferring.'

In an effort to alleviate the situation Nicole spread her hands wide and rationalised, 'It's just that it seems to imply....'

'What? That that's where my orders originate? Well, so they do. Or are you now of the opinion that I shouldn't take orders from him either?'

'No, of course not! I only meant....' With a deprecatory hunching of her shoulder she stopped and grimaced wryly. This wasn't getting either of them anywhere. 'Oh, Dad, don't let's argue. I'm sorry if I jumped to conclusions, it's just that I'd never heard the saying before, that's all.'

'On top of which, it was impossible for you to pass up the chance to have another dig at Lang.'

'That too, I guess,' she half laughed ruefully.

'But why, Nicky?'

'I'm not sure really,' she shrugged. 'Perhaps because he reminds me of Jerome.'

'Reminds you of ...! He's nothing at all like him!' Bryce expostulated.

'Oh, I wasn't meaning in looks.'

'Neither was I,' caustically.

'But he does remind me of Jerome's and my break-up. He was at the flat when it all happened, you see.'

'So was I, but I don't keep making you remember, do I?' he frowned in puzzlement.

'No, but then I expected to have to tell you the whole story. What I didn't bargain for was having a complete stranger there to hear it as well,' she explained with considerable dryness.

At the disgruntled look on her face Bryce began to smile. 'I would hardly have thought that was sufficient reason for disliking the man,' he argued persuasively.

Probably not, *if* that was all there was to it, Nicole agreed silently. But as she had no intention of revealing the exact state of her feelings—she wasn't even confident she knew that herself!—she merely made an indecisive movement with her shoulders which was partly acquiescent and partly defensive and changed the subject by suggesting,

'If you're ready, perhaps we'd better have lunch.'

They shared a desultory conversation during the meal, most of it centring around Nicole's experiences in Nullegai, but when she rose to make the coffee afterwards and her father began clearing the table and stacking the plates in the sink, she remembered a question she had meant to ask earlier and flashed him a quizzical look while plugging in the kettle.

'How come you've been having your meals up there?' A nod of her head was directed towards the large white house in the distance. 'That's not the normal practice, is it?'

'On a lot of stations it is,' she was told matter-of-factly. 'It all depends.'

The arch of Nicole's brows became more pronounced. 'On what?'

Bryce exhaled a deep breath and leant back leisurely in his chair. 'Circumstances,' he smiled uninformatively, but went on to explain, 'Such as the attitude of the owner, the size of the homestead and the property, the number of employees, convenience ... oh, any number of things. But to answer your question, no, it is not unusual to find unmarried jackaroos, overseers, book-keepers etcetera, sharing the owner's board.'

'Very democratic!' Nicole couldn't control the facetious quip which immediately sprang to mind, but when her father showed signs of remonstrating, covered it swiftly with a less provoking, 'At least it's good news to know you don't have to bother getting your own meals.'

'Yes, well ...' He paused, looking decidedly uneasy, then proposed, 'And—er—now to the bad news.'

'Such as?' she frowned warily.

'The invitation I issued to Lang to have dinner with us tonight,' came the dry admission which had Nicole staring at him in dismay.

'Oh, Dad, you didn't!' she reproached. 'Whatever for?'

'Because I considered it would be a nice gesture seeing that Jessie Verdon, his cook-cum-housekeeper, won't be here tonight, and,' he fixed her with a significant glance, 'because I thought you would have overcome that misplaced animosity of yours by now.'

The implied criticism Nicole allowed to pass unchallenged. She had more pressing matters on her mind.

'But someone has to feed the rest of the men who usually have their meals in the homestead, don't they? Why can't he eat with them?' she demanded. 'Or are you saying that the three of us will be the only ones on the place tonight?' A somewhat daunting thought!

'No, Alan and Sandy, two of the married station hands, will be here too, although I'm sure that, unlike you, either of their wives would be most happy to have Lang join them for a meal.'

'So why didn't they ask him then?'

'Because it was only when he offered to bring you back to Yallambee with him that anyone knew he would be here for dinner,' he advised heavily. 'Like most of the single men, I gather, he normally stays in town on Saturday nights.'

With his wealthy contemporary Eunice Blanchard, no doubt, surmised Nicole acidly. It was a pity he hadn't kept to the same routine for this Saturday too! It was also a shame someone else hadn't forestalled her father's bigheartedness with a prior invitation! Moodily she filled the waiting cups with the now boiling water and carried them to the table.

'Well, I hope he isn't expecting anything elaborate,' she ventured finally after a long silence. 'I don't aim to spend the whole of my afternoon slaving in the kitchen just for his benefit.'

'Nicky!' Her father's voice carried a thread of warning. 'No one has asked you to go to that much trouble. Actually, I thought a roast would probably be the easiest for you, so I asked Jessie if she could take a leg of pork out of the deep freeze this morning.'

It was starting to sound better. It would only take five minutes to prepare the vegetables to accompany it.

'You've got enough apples for the sauce?' she enquired quickly. During her earlier explorations she hadn't noticed any.

'Not here,' he smiled. 'But Jessie said you would be wanting some, so she was going to leave those out for you with the meat. She also said that if it made things easier,' he cleared his throat deliberately as if preparing himself for what he knew was to come, 'to feel free to use her kitchen instead.'

'What? Up there?' Nicole asked incredulously, and rejected the offer just as rapidly. 'Uh-uh, this is good enough for me. If the kitchen is on the same scale as the house I'd probably get lost going from one side of the room to the other!'

'You're sure?'

Nicole looked at him steadily over the rim of her cup, her eyes gleaming. 'What do you think?' she laughed irrepressibly.

'I think you're one mixed-up young lady who's likely to reap the proverbial whirlwind if you're not very careful,' he retorted in kind. 'Judging by what I've seen of him, Lang Jamieson would be a pretty tough customer should he decide to take you to task for all your deliberate riling.'

Her chin angled higher. 'And don't you think I could stay the distance?'

'You might be stubborn, Nicky, but you're not a fool, and that's what you would be if you try,' he admonished seriously.

'Oh, well, we'll have to wait and see, won't we?' Nicole smiled, only not quite so sanguinely as before, and took her cup over to the sink. 'Meanwhile ... if I start on the dishes, would you mind very much collecting the meat and apples from the house for me?'

Bryce brought his own cup over to her and gave

her a gentle tug with his free hand. 'After the comments you've been making I don't think I'd dare let you get them yourself. Perhaps the less you two see of each other the better.'

'Our thoughts are in tune at last,' she approved on a dramatic sigh. 'I knew you'd come round to my way of thinking in the end.'

'Not all the way,' he cautioned firmly. 'Just remember, he *is* my boss and, contrary to what you may have persuaded yourself into believing, I fully intend to see that you show him some respect while you're here.'

Nicole wrinkled her nose at him in mock disappointment. 'I never really supposed otherwise,' she confessed candidly.

The washing up was finished and Nicole was putting away the last of their dishes by the time Bryce returned from the homestead and on seeing what he had brought back with him Nicole made a mental note to thank Jessie Verdon for the trouble she had taken on their behalf when she met that lady. Not only had she left the meat for them but she had pared all the vegetables and left them too. White potatoes and sweet potatoes, baby carrots, beans and peas, and instead of crisp green apples to peel and slice there was a jar of freshly made apple sauce. All that remained was to cook them and make a nice rich gravy.

As soon as the meat was in the oven and the heat turned down low, Nicole made for her bedroom to change into an old pair of jeans and a tomato red sleeveless top. She pushed her feet into sneakers and tied her hair back from her face with the aid of a chiffon scarf and, after remembering to collect a towelling beach hat and her sunglasses, she rejoined her father in the sitting room.

Because of the limited time at their disposal for an inspection of the property they had decided on one of the motorbikes as the quickest way to travel, and Nicole was looking forward to it. Clark Rutherford, Cynthia's husband, had owned a bike when they first met and on a number of occasions he had taken Nicole as a pillion passenger for the experience—much to her enjoyment.

Their first stop wasn't very far from the cottage, a small paddock behind the shearing shed where Sable and her newborn calf were being held temporarily. The calf was curled up in the grass dozing contentedly when they reached him, his curly black hide warm from the sun, one twitching ear defeating the efforts of a fly to settle on it.

'Oh, Dad, he's gorgeous!' Nicole exclaimed as she went down on her knees beside the small form and ran her hand over the soft hair. 'What's he called, or don't you give calves names?'

Completing his scrutiny of Sable, who was watching the proceedings closely from the corners of her big soulful brown eyes, Bryce dropped to his haunches beside her and nodded.

'He will have—he's a purebred,' he advised. 'He'll

no doubt be Yallambee Jupiter something or other, the same as his sire.'

'Good lord, and here was I thinking he was just a plain old calf,' she laughed. 'My imagination wasn't envisaging anything quite so grand, I'm sorry to say. I was thinking along more prosaic lines ... such as Blackie, or—or Curly.'

'Mmm,' Bryce smiled along with her. 'But you'll find his pedigree name will suit him better when he's fully grown. Don't forget, he won't be this cute for long. That's a ton or more of muscle and bone in the making, you know.'

'Yes, I suppose so,' she conceded, and eyed the placid form lying in the grass with new respect. In a couple of years' time he would probably make his dam, who had now come forward to lick at him roughly, look like a midget. Rising agilely to her feet, Nicole dusted off her jeans and turned to her father enquiringly.

'Where to now?' she asked.

'That way,' he pointed across undulating grasslands to a tree and hill-blurred horizon as they walked back to the bike. 'Then I can check on the water tanks and troughs as we go.'

'But I thought you were supposed to have finished work for the day,' Nicole protested in astonishment.

'So I have ... as far as it goes,' he shrugged equably. 'Although caring for animals is hardly comparable to a nine-to-five office job, love, and while we're on the property I guess none of us is altogether off duty. There's always something that can go wrong.'

A point Nicole hadn't considered before and which she now acknowledged with an understanding nod. 'So it's part of your job to check they have enough water, is it?' she quizzed as she swung on to the bike behind him.

'Not exactly, but it is my responsibility to see they don't run out, and there's a considerable difference in those requirements if you care to look for it,' he grinned at her over his shoulder. 'In actual fact, they're checked just about every morning, but as I was planning to take you in that direction anyway I didn't think it would hurt to have a look for myself.'

She should have known, Nicole smiled wryly to herself. No one could possibly have been more conscientious towards their work than her father, and if that meant combining work with pleasure during his free time then he would do it willingly.

As it happened, it was fortunate he had decided to check again that day, because a calf from Yallambee's commercial herd had become bogged in the muddy sides of one of the earthen water tanks they visited, and due to its struggles it was only just strong enough to stand when Bryce managed to get it back on its feet again. Had it been left till the following morning it was doubtful it would have survived.

The country they passed through was entirely different from that which Nicole had seen on the drive from town. Gone were the waving fields of grain and in their place were quite heavily wooded hills and hollows where emus and kangaroos seemed to share the paddocks with sheep or cattle with equal familiarity.

By the time they had wound their way along one boundary and down on to the flats again the hour was fast approaching for Nicole to add some of the vegetables to their roast, and as they cut back towards the homestead Bryce continued straight on to the cottage instead of stopping so they could inspect the grain silos as had originally been intended.

'Well, that's that,' Nicole remarked a while later as she viewed the cooking food with satisfaction through the oven's glass door. 'Now all that needs to be done is to put the peas and beans on after I've showered and get the....' Her expression turned to one of dismay as she closed her eyes tightly and finished on a frantic note, '*Dessert!* I forgot the dessert!' A pleading glance at her father, and, 'Is there anything suitable I could use in the cupboard? I haven't really got time to make anything.'

His broad shoulders rose unhelpfully. 'You would probably know that better than I would, love,' he replied. 'But if there isn't, you don't have to worry about it, I'm sure it won't hurt any of us to miss out on dessert for a night.'

What? And give Lang the opportunity to make some disparaging comment? Not likely!

Nicole dismissed his remark with a vigorous shake of her head and, flinging open the pantry door, began moving tins and packets around on the shelves. At last she gave a relieved sigh and brought forth a jar of brandied peaches. They had been included on the spur of the moment when she had packed her father's groceries because his birthday wasn't far away and she had planned to use them for a special meal she proposed making. What to serve with them, though? They needed something!

'You don't suppose Jessie would have some cream in her fridge that we could borrow, do you?' she enquired with bated breath.

Bryce's response was definitely more encouraging this time. 'Oh, if that's all you want there's no problem.' He glanced at his watch and explained, 'Sandy's probably doing the milking about now and his eldest daughter will put some through the separator for you. I'll ride down and get it while you're having your shower, shall I?'

'Please!' Her eyes glowed with appreciation.

Raising one finger to his temple, Bryce took his departure and Nicole headed gratefully for the bathroom. It had been hot and dusty on the bike and a cool shower was going to be very welcome.

Afterwards, feeling very much refreshed, she hurried back to her room to begin dressing. And that was where the trouble started. As she had only expected to have her father for company over the week-

end she hadn't bothered bringing a dress, apart from
the one she had travelled in, and seeing that was
somewhat creased she didn't feel like wearing it
again. With a sigh and a wry grimace she stared for
some minutes at the meagre contents of the wardrobe
and then shrugged. Oh, well, there was nothing for it
but to wear the royal blue slacks and pearl blue
stretch tank top. It wasn't exactly what one would
call dressy, but it was the best she could do on such
short notice and with so little to choose from.

Next came a touch of eyeshadow and mascara, followed by a pale pink lipstick, and then she parted her
hair in the middle and brushed it back behind her
ears so that it continued in a straight fall past her
shoulders. The sound of the gauze door slamming in
the kitchen had her taking one final check in the
mirror and heading in that direction.

On the threshold she stopped, suddenly flustered
on seeing Lang in the room with her father. She
hadn't expected his arrival this early and the impact
his unanticipated appearance had on her was, as it
had been on the two previous occasions, startling. In
a matter of seconds her mind registered a host of details. Hip-hugging bottle green pants, cream silk
knit shirt which made his skin appear incredibly
dark, damp curling hair, the faint aroma of a spicy
aftershave, coolly alert twany eyes, and an uncom-
promising set to his normally well curved mouth.
Unable to withdraw her gaze, she felt her heart plum-

met to the vicinity of her knees and back again. Oh, hell, she despaired, it was going to be one of *those* nights!

When she finally managed to murmur a greeting it was embarrassingly awkward, but Lang's brusque return did nothing to settle the winging butterflies which had taken control of her stomach and she moved into the room with all the apparent enthusiasm of someone attending their own funeral.

'Oh, good, you're ready, Nicky,' her father said, hearing her voice, and turned from where he had been extracting some glasses from the cabinet above the divider which separated the kitchen from the dining room. 'You can entertain Lang while I have my shower. I ran into him at Sandy's and suggested he might as well came back with me.' Opening the fridge door to retrieve a tray of ice which he tipped into an anodised bucket and then transferred some to one of the glasses, he nodded to a rose-patterned jug on the top shelf. 'Your cream's in there,' he smiled.

Literally sidling past where Lang stood, Nicole stammered, 'Oh—er—thanks, Dad,' and flew towards the sink where she began tipping the beans and peas into their respective saucepans and filling them with water. 'I'll get these on and then dinner will be just about ready by the time you are,' she chattered nervously.

'Right,' he replied easily, apparently unaware of her unaccustomed agitation as he poured a generous amount of whisky over the ice in the glass and handed it to their guest before asking, 'How about you, love? Would you like a drink while you're waiting?'

Something to settle her nerves? It sounded a great idea!

'Sherry, please,' she answered as gaily as she could, and took a quick mouthful immediately the filled glass was placed in her hand. Not that it seemed to have a particularly beneficial effect. All she had now was a warm stomach to match her already warm face!

Once her father had left Nicole crossed to the oven hotplates, set the two saucepans down and turned the appropriate control knobs, then swung to face Lang edgily.

'I'm sorry, won't you please take a seat,' she indicated those about the kitchen and dining room tables. 'Or if you would prefer, there's a television in the sitting room,' waving a hand towards the room on the opposite side of the hall. A rather superfluous statement, she decided promptly, since it was he who had furnished the cottage in the first place.

Deliberately, Lang drained the contents of his glass, placed it firmly on the table and held her wary gaze with a resolute one.

'Look, I'm well aware you had no part in this invitation and if it's any consolation to you I wasn't particularly anxious to accept it, but I did so out of regard for your father. However, if it's going to have you behaving like a neurotic cat on hot bricks all evening then I think it's best for all concerned if I leave,' he told her curtly.

'No!' Nicole burst out, aghast, as he took a step towards the door, and involuntarily grabbed hold of his arm to stop him. Dear God, her father would never forgive her! 'Don't you dare,' she ordered fiercely, finding a rising anger at his derisive description to be a far more satisfactory nerve-soother than her sherry had been. 'You accepted the invitation and now you can abide by it. You're not going to use me as an excuse to leave.'

'No?' Black-lashed eyes goaded aggravatingly.

'No!'

His glance dropped pointedly to the hand still clutching his arm. 'Are you intending to use force in an attempt to stop me?' he taunted.

Red banners of humiliation tinted Nicole's cheeks and she released him as if she had suddenly found herself holding something lethal. 'I'm sorry,' she whispered stiffly, miserably. Her father would never believe she hadn't intentionally brought about Lang's departure. In the background the water in the shower was turned off and with a growing sense of panic she was reluctantly impelled into entreating, 'Please don't leave. Dad would be terribly upset.'

'With whom?'

Seconds ticked by during which Nicole's temper started climbing again. As if he needed to be told!

'With me, of course!' she finally admitted with a resentful glare.

A considering look crossed Lang's face and he rocked back on his heels with an insolent grace. 'So my presence is worth a considerable amount to you at the moment, right?'

'In a manner of speaking,' she agreed uneasily. Just what was he getting at?

'And in order to ensure it you would be prepared to come to terms, wouldn't you, kitten?' he drawled lazily.

Now she could see which way his thoughts were headed and her breathing deepened uncontrollably. 'What sort of terms?' she seethed impotently, as aware as he that she wasn't in a position to argue.

One eyebrow crooked in simulated amazement. 'Can't you guess?'

'Something to the effect that I should treat you with honoured deference and obeisance as befits your position and wealth?' she gibed derisively.

Lang's eyes slid over her in cool appraisal. 'A permanent restraint on that temperamental and acrimonious nature of yours would suffice,' he retorted bitingly. 'Or don't you believe in keeping to any agreements you make?'

Nicole flicked a loose tendril of hair back impatiently over her shoulder. 'If you're referring to this morning, I only agreed for the sake of the Club to keep my personal feelings separate from any working relationship we had, Lang, not to forget them altogether.'

'Then I suggest it's time you did.'

'And if I don't, you'll refuse to stay, is that it?'

'More or less,' he concurred sardonically.

'Because you can't take it, or because no one's ever allowed to oppose the all-powerful Lang Jamieson ... just as a matter of principle?' she jeered scornfully.

The indifferent flexing of wide shoulders she received in response was in complete variance to the glittering fury evident in Lang's amber eyes, but the result was disastrous from Nicole's standpoint. Without a word he pushed open the screen door which led on to the back verandah and walked out.

Dismay clouded Nicole's features as she stood momentarily staring at the place where he had last been and then, turning down the elements on the hotplates to a simmering temperature, she hastily chased after him.

'Lang! You're not being fair!' she protested to his fast disappearing form in the inky blackness. But when he showed no sign of halting she had, perforce, to stumble further along the path to the homestead in pursuit.

'Lang! Please!' she called again, managing to come within a few feet of him, and when he still showed no sign of slowing or turning, 'All right! I apologise for what I said and I'll agree to whatever terms you like, only please come back to the house. Dad will never speak to me again if you don't,' she ended on a mournfully defeated sigh.

At last he swung to face her, but it was far too dark for Nicole to read his expression and she listened to his satiric questioning, 'Whatever terms I like?' with apprehensive shivers rippling down her spine.

'Well ... within reason,' she qualified shakily.

He uttered a short bark of mocking laughter. 'What gives you the idea I would be interested in any that weren't?' he derided coldly. 'As far as I'm aware, all I've asked for from you is sociability! Anything else you might be tempted to credit me with is purely a figment of your own imagination, I can assure you!'

The feeling that she had been deliberately led into that snubbing barrage remained even as Nicole's cheeks burned at the disparagement his words contained and she set about defending herself with as much dignity as possible.

'That's a relief,' she returned just as icily. 'It's pleasing to know that in one direction at least we're in total accord.'

'And the others?'

She shrugged with a studied nonchalance although she doubted he could see the offhand gesture in the dark. 'If those are your terms then I have no alternative but to say butter will not melt in my mouth in future. In fact,' she paused and her lips pursed pleasurably, 'I could even become so sweet you'll find it sickening.'

'I doubt it,' he discounted laconically. 'The change will be too refreshing.' A firm hand caught hold of her upper arm to turn her towards the cottage. 'But now that's settled, perhaps we'd better go. Your father will be wondering where we are.'

A circumstance which hadn't appeared to cause him any concern until after he had managed to get exactly what he wanted, Nicole noted furiously, and swiftly removed her arm from his grasp. Whatever else he was, Lang Jamieson was well on his way to becoming an expert at turning her misfortunes to his own advantage!

Fortunately for Nicole her father hadn't emerged from his bedroom before they re-entered the kitchen —she hadn't been looking forward to explaining why they had been missing—and she was able to proceed with the remainder of the preparations for the meal and to lay the table in the dining room without any further interruptions.

CHAPTER FIVE

WHILE dinner was in progress Nicole said very little, being preoccupied with her own thoughts in the main, and only contributing to the men's conversation when a remark was addressed directly to her. Her father was obviously pleased with what he surmised to be her voluntary change of heart with regard to Lang, for her manner towards him couldn't have been faulted, but her own feelings ran along less satisfied lines.

As she had pointed out to her father earlier in the day, their guest's presence recalled Jerome to mind, but even more distressing than the recollection was the way in which Lang's image constantly supplanted itself so inexorably over the other, and she was at something of a loss to understand why. Jerome had been the man she loved, the man she had anticipated marrying, and yet Lang was the one who always seemed to be in her thoughts. So far, the only explanation she had been able to proffer for such contrariness was that her animosity towards him was such an instinctive emotion that it completely obliterated all others. Further than that she saw no reason to delve at present.

Once the meal—which to Nicole's relief had been cooked to a turn—was concluded and the time came to clear away the dishes, she was surprised to find Lang calmly sharing the honours with her father and drying the plates as she washed them. Not that she didn't think him capable of drying a pot or pan—it wasn't an exercise which required a great deal of expertise—but in view of his background she had expected him to consider it too lowly a task for him to perform.

Had their positions been reversed she knew Jerome would never have offered, not even, 'In repayment for your hospitality,' as Lang had declared in response to her protest that he didn't have to bother, because Jerome had always been extremely conscious of position and what he considered to be either above or below it. To his credit, Lang clearly didn't attach much importance to such considerations.

'By the way,' his voice suddenly broke in on her reverie, 'I have some circulars in my office which Avril Maher, the Club Secretary, had copied and sent out to all members. I intended bringing them with me this evening, but through meeting your father at Sandy's I didn't go back to the house again. I'll bring them down to you in the morning, or,' the corners of his eyes crinkled disarmingly, 'if you feel like taking a dip in the pool then you might prefer to collect them yourself.'

'Thank you,' Nicole nodded her acknowledgment

of his offer, although she doubted she would be taking him up on it. She hadn't the slightest wish to feel indebted to him. However, since viewing his home that morning she had experienced a certain curiosity to see whether the interior equalled its imposing exterior and made the excuse, 'Yes, well I might call for them, if you don't mind, as I wanted to thank Mrs Verdon for having left the dinner vegetables all prepared.'

Bryce finished stacking some of the clean plates in the cupboard and returned to take up his tea towel. 'How did you become interested in the Swimming Club in the first place, Lang?' he asked. 'I would have thought you had enough to do running Yallambee without taking on more.'

'Oh, I don't know,' came the casual reply with a shrug. 'It's a sport I've always enjoyed myself and as I moved the original motion at the Council meeting with regard to building a pool in Nullegai, I just felt I ought to follow the project through. Actually, I didn't intend to become involved with the Swimming Club when it was formed—my main objective had been the pool itself—but I went along to the first meeting out of interest and suddenly found myself being elected into office,' he recalled wryly.

'You could have declined the nomination if you didn't want it,' Nicole pointed out subtly, wishing he had.

'I could,' he acceded ironically. 'But as no one else

seemed overly anxious to take on the position then I figured someone had to if the Club was to get moving at all.'

A situation Nicole could well imagine. She had seen the same thing happen before. Everyone wanted the benefits, but it was always left to the same few to do all the work.

'And the first time trials are to be held this Wednesday, is that right?' she enquired.

'Uh-huh!' His lips curved ruefully. 'Sorry, I should have told you before, Avril asked me to. She's been away for the last couple of weeks, otherwise I expect she would have been round to see you before this.'

Nicole nodded in understanding. She had thought it a little strange that no one from the Club had been in touch with her, but that explained it.

'Qualifying times and distances, have they already been settled too?' she asked.

'Yes, Avril had a few discussions with the coach in Franklyn and we've decided to follow their lead. Under thirty seconds for thirty metres and they have to go up to fifty metres, and so on.'

'So all that remains now is to get our stopwatches out and see who's capable of doing what,' she smiled.

'That's about it,' he returned with a lazy grin that had Nicole swallowing convulsively in an effort to counteract its calamitous effect. 'Have you got any surprises in store?'

She leant her head to one side and angled him a

scheming glance. 'Could be,' she allowed mysteriously, thinking of young Rhonda Parrish's rapid progress. 'You'll just have to wait until Wednesday to find out, won't you?'

'As you obviously aren't going to tell me, do I have any option?' His brows peaked graphically.

'No,' she smiled down at the pan she was scrubbing. It would, no doubt, be something of a change for him not to know everything that was happening!

They retired to the sitting room after the washing up was completed and the conversation became more general, but by the time Lang took his leave Nicole was more than ready to seek her own bed—the day had been eventful in a number of ways—and wishing her father goodnight she thankfully made her way to her room.

The friendly, though raucous, laughter of a pair of kookaburras perched in the tree beside her bedroom window brought Nicole back to consciousness and a bright new day filled with clear warm sunlight and the delicious aroma of cooking bacon. Leaning across to her bedside table she picked up her watch and gasped audibly when she saw the time. It was half past eight already and she had anticipated being awake long before this. Swiftly she swung her shapely tanned legs over the side of the bed and hurried along to the bathroom to clean her teeth and wash before donning a pair of bronze shorts and a strapless lemon cotton top.

'You should have woken me,' she reproached her father lightly as she entered the kitchen to find him halfway through his breakfast, a book propped up against the condiment set in front of him. 'I didn't intend to sleep for so long.'

Bryce looked up with a smile. 'There was no rush,' he replied evenly. 'I figured you must have needed it.'

Nicole poured herself a cup of coffee and took the seat opposite him at the table.

'Yes, well, I didn't want to waste the little time we do have together these days by spending it all in bed,' she remarked wryly, and began spreading butter on a slice of toast left in the rack. 'Especially since I have to see Mrs Verdon, as well as collect those papers from Lang this morning.'

'You can do that after breakfast while I have a word with Alan and Sandy about what needs doing today,' he suggested, closing his book and placing it on the divider behind him. 'That will give you time to have your swim, see Lang and Jessie—who should be back by then—and meet me here afterwards.'

As her father would have thought it extremely odd if Nicole had told him she didn't intend accepting Lang's offer to use his pool she said nothing in return, merely making a vague movement with her head as if in acceptance. Perhaps she could fill in the extra time he was obviously expecting her to be away by talking to Jessie Verdon.

The path which led to the homestead was well worn and Nicole had no trouble following it past the shrubs at the edge of the gardens some thirty minutes later after leaving her father to continue on his way to find Alan and Sandy. The sun was pleasantly warm on her shoulders and as she was in no hurry she sauntered slowly between the trees and bushes, inhaling appreciatively as the varied perfumes assailed her senses.

Closer to the homestead the path became a wide walkway beneath a vine-covered pergola where shadows drew a delicate tracery on the cool flagstones and a garden table and chairs stood waiting for occupancy in their leafy green arbour. The swimming pool, she inadvertently found, was situated on a terrace at the back of the house, its long length decidedly inviting as the water glistened brightly under a clear blue sky.

A hasty check in all directions showed no one about and Nicole couldn't resist slipping across to it. On the pebble-decked edge she slid her right foot out of its sandal and bent to test the temperature with her toes. As she had suspected, it was gloriously warm.

'You're just in time to join me.'

Lang's voice so close behind her had her spinning out of her crouching position rapidly. Too rapidly. The heel of her other sandal caught against the lip of the pool and with a surprised gasp she overbalanced, falling backwards into the water with a resounding splash.

Surfacing almost immediately, she swept her hair away from her face and gazed down at her soaked clothes with chagrin. 'Now look at me!' she wailed. 'You might at least have let me know you were coming!'

From his vantage point above her Lang gave no indication of penitence. 'If you're that jittery perhaps you should consider holding on to the rails in future,' he suggested sardonically.

'I wouldn't need to if you didn't creep up on me!'

Just to see him standing there, his own navy blue swimming shorts dry and a towel slung casually around his neck, was enough to have Nicole's temper flaring.

'I did not creep up on you,' he denied coolly, bending over to offer her an outstretched hand. 'I was already on my way out here when I saw you walking across the terrace.'

'Well, I couldn't see you,' she retorted and, after only a moment's hesitation, placed her hand in his. The steps *were* right at the other end of the pool.

Her other hand she placed on the side in order to steady and help push herself up, but as she did so the weight of water in her strapless top had it slipping relentlessly downwards and she made a frantic grab for it. The result was a hard and totally unexpected jerk on the hand Lang was holding which had him half falling, half diving, into the pool beside her.

Poetic justice, chuckled Nicole, and grinned broadly to see the towel, now sodden, still clinging to him as his head and shoulders came into view again.

'You little...!' He broke off furiously and tossed the towel unceremoniously up on the side. 'I was trying to help you!'

'I know,' she laughed, but on seeing the look on his face as he pushed through the water towards her, and suddenly realising he believed she had done it on purpose, began protesting, 'I didn't mean to do it, Lang! Honestly, I didn't!'

'The hell you didn't! You've been dying to get back at me ever since we met!'

'But not this time,' she disclaimed with a smiling shake of her head. 'Besides, I don't know what you're complaining about—at least you're dressed for it.'

'Which makes it acceptable, I suppose?'

'No, but....'

Nicole began backing away as fast as she could. Her not being able to resist smiling at the memory wasn't helping to convince him of her innocence in the slightest and, when it became apparent he would reach her before she could make it to the steps and safety, she turned quickly and started swimming. Half a dozen strokes showed her the futility of her attempt because she had to stop again to hurriedly hitch her top back into position and by that time a heavy hand had descended on to her shoulder and swung her around.

'I'm sorry, Lang, but I really didn't do it on purpose,' she swiftly tried to appease him.

'Mmm, and I'm not doing this on purpose either!' he retorted, unimpressed, as a hand wrapped itself within the darkened strands of her hair and his head bent to hers.

Nicole had no chance to demur before she was crushed to a hard chest and his mouth covered hers in angry chastisement. She wanted to fight, even began to, but the warmth of his lips aroused traitorous emotions reminiscent of another time when he had held her in much the same way and, quite without thinking, she found herself relaxing against him and responding to his stirring domination without restraint.

With the fading of her token resistance Lang's hold became less punishing and his mouth more persuasive. His hands slid slowly over her back to rest on the slender curves of her waist where shorts and top had briefly parted company and Nicole could feel the hardness of solid muscle pressed against her from breast to thigh. Lost to all but the need to return his embraces, her own hands moved experimentally over the powerfully ridged chest to clutch at broad shoulders as his kisses deepened.

She couldn't quite believe what was happening, yet she was unable to break away. Her blood was racing through her body like a river in flood and the pounding of her heart was deafening to her ears. She didn't know why he should have been capable of exercising such a hypnotic control over her emotions, but at the same time she seemed powerless to deny it.

Finally raising his dark head, Lang looked steadily down into her bemused blue eyes. 'That was a pretty convincing exhibition, wasn't it, for someone who's reputedly sworn off men for life?' he taunted roughly. 'Or were you just playing substitutes again?'

Inwardly shrinking away from the derision in his tone, Nicole shrugged carelessly. 'No more than you were,' she gibed, suddenly remembering Eunice Blanchard. She only wished she had thought of her before. That could have been what she needed to put a brake on her compliance.

'Meaning?'

She gave another shrug and began heading for the steps. 'Only that you must have women friends of your own you would rather have been devoting your attentions to.'

He didn't deny it, only going on to demand, 'And the reason for your response? I still haven't heard that yet.'

'Mine?' She forced a laugh and eyed him flippantly. 'Oh, that's easy. As your kisses were clearly meant as a form of punishment I decided to disarm you, that's all. There are many ways of winning, you know, Lang, not the least of which is by appearing to lose!'

The look she received in response was a cold and contemptuous one and she clambered up the steps with more haste than grace to escape his discomfiting presence.

'I'll—I'll come back for the—for the papers later,' she stammered on reaching firm ground again. 'You stay and have your swim.'

'No, thanks, I seem to have lost the desire for it,' he bit out as he came to stand beside her. 'And you may as well collect the papers. That is what you came for, isn't it?'

'Yes, but there's no hurry, I can pick them up some time this afternoon just as easily.'

'You'll do it now, or not at all,' he told her arrogantly. 'I won't be here this afternoon.'

'Well, in that case....' She hunched one shoulder awkwardly, but Lang had already turned on his heel, striding for the homestead, and she had no choice but to follow him reluctantly. At the kitchen door she hung back, uncomfortably aware of the water still dripping from her clothes. 'I'll wait for you here,' she suggested. 'I don't want to make a mess of the floors.'

'Oh, for God's sake, stop making damned excuses!' A hand gripped her wrist ungently and pulled her through the doorway. 'I have no intention of kissing you again, if that's what's bothering you.'

'It isn't—it's a genuine concern for someone else's property!' she rounded on him resentfully, glaring at his bronzed back as she was hauled speedily through a polished pine and lime-tiled kitchen, their passage leaving a trail of water on the glazed brick flooring.

'Don't worry, it's had water dropped on it before,' he revealed drily, his head turning for a brief glance. 'It may look like a showplace, but it's a home first.'

Wryly, Nicole decided that such a casual regard could only come from a lifelong association. From what she could see as they travelled down the hallway and into a book-lined study the whole place shouted a refined wealth and expense which made her over-whelmingly aware of the difference in their life-styles. What he considered commonplace she was admiring in silent awe.

From the second drawer of a leather-inlaid desk Lang extracted a sheaf of papers and motioned towards the door.

'I'll go over these with you in the kitchen,' he said, and suddenly grinned. 'I haven't had breakfast yet.'

Nicole swallowed quickly and looked away. That smile of his continually set her off balance. 'I won't keep you, then,' she murmured nervously. 'I can look through them at the cottage, after I've changed.'

'No, there's a couple of details Avril asked me to explain to you, so we'd better do it together,' he over-ruled her opposition calmly on the way back to the kitchen. 'However,' his eyes flicked over her dishevelled appearance in lazy amusement, if you would like something a little less damp to change into I'm sure I could find something one of my sisters has left behind which would be suitable while we put yours through the dryer.'

A little less damp, and a little less revealing, Nicole grimaced. Now that most of the water had drained from them her shorts and top were clinging to her like a second skin. But it would be easier, and a good deal more calming, if she could just leave altogether! To her mortification she was finding she wasn't entirely unaffected by his state of dress, or rather undress, either!

'No, no, there's no need to go to so much trouble,' she protested. 'I can. . . .'

'Sit down and do as you're told for a change,' he ordered peremptorily with a firm hand on her shoulder pushing her down on to one of the chairs at the kitchen table to enforce the command. 'I won't be long.'

Nicole sighed in vexation but stayed seated. There wasn't much else she could do, seeing he had made certain he took the papers with him to forestall an early departure on her part.

When he returned he was carrying a pale blue and white patterned housecoat, a towel, and brush and comb which he handed over to her. Gratefully she noted that he had changed too, into a clean bush shirt and matching drill pants which were secured about his lean waist with a wide leather belt.

'There's another bathroom off the laundry,' he indicated a door at the end of the kitchen. 'If you like, you can change there instead of going all the way upstairs.'

Glad to be free of his disturbing personality for even a short while, Nicole hurried to do as he suggested. Clad in dry clothes—even though they hinted at an intimacy she would rather have avoided—and with her hair towelled and combed neatly, she felt better able to continue. Her wet outfit she placed in the dryer and set it going herself on the way back to the table.

Lang was occupied with a frypan on the bench when she re-entered the room and he turned to face her with a look of enquiry.

'Have you eaten?'

'Yes, thanks,' she nodded, and stood watching indecisively as he flipped an egg in the pan. 'Is there anything I—I can do to help?'

'Uh-uh, everything's under control,' he drawled. 'However, if your housewifely inclinations really need to be pacified, you could attend to the coffee.'

Nicole ignored the sarcasm and moved towards the bubbling percolator, pleased to have something to do other than watch him. When she did that her thoughts strangely became very wayward and difficult to control.

'Will you pour, or shall I?' she asked a few minutes later after they had taken their seats at the table.

'It's all yours, kitten,' Lang shrugged indolently,

thanking her when she handed him his cup before pouring her own. 'Are you sure you won't have anything to eat?'

She half smiled and shook her head. 'No, thanks, I had mine some time ago. Aren't you a little late with yours?' Her blue eyes gleamed irrepressibly.

'A little,' he agreed lazily. 'But then I didn't get back from my morning round until shortly before you arrived.'

'You've been working already?'

'Just checking up on a few things.'

'My father's work?' The caustic question slipped out before Nicole realised what she was saying.

'Not particularly.' One dark eyebrow angled upwards annoyingly. 'Should I have been?'

Nicole stared down at her coffee miserably, wishing she had never made the remark. If she wasn't careful she would be putting doubts in his mind regarding her father's ability.

'No, of course not,' she spoke at last, her gaze joining his uneasily. She couldn't quite fathom what his reaction had been. 'I only meant. . . .'

'To have a gibe at me, not to cast any slur on your parent.'

'I'm sorry,' she apologised dismally, chewing at a soft bottom lip. 'I shouldn't have said it.'

'I'll second that!'

Lang's concurrence came in such a low, taut tone that Nicole sought to ease the tension by reminding him, 'The Club papers. You said there were some points to be explained?'

For a time he didn't answer, merely holding her gaze which was unknowingly pleading. Then he expelled a heavy breath, his expression, much to Nicole's relief, turning wry.

'I sometimes wonder if you quite realise how close you come to actually being made to suffer the consequences for those goading comments of yours,' he reflected.

'I thought I already had!'

'By our agreement?' he laughed shortly. 'That's only a minor infringement compared to some I would consider appropriate.'

Nicole thought it neither judicious nor prudent to seek elucidation on the point and gave her undivided attention to the typed sheets on the table between them instead. Right at the moment she needed something other than herself to engage his interest.

Pointing swiftly to the top page, she enquired, 'Is this what Avril meant? The schedule of the racing carnivals?'

Finally he nodded. 'Together with the procedures on the Club's race nights. Mostly they're scratch races, but occasionally they're handicap. That way it gives even the slower swimmers at least a chance of winning, and it makes the faster ones put that little bit extra into their efforts.'

Now that they were discussing her favourite subject Nicole found it easy to temporarily discard her antagonism where Lang was concerned and converse with a willingness which obviously came as a surprise to the man beside her. Distances, strokes, training, competitions, number of members, and the billeting necessary when visiting teams stayed in town or when Nullegai's members went away were all discussed at length and with accord. With so much amiability, in fact, that Nicole was totally unaware of the time passing and it wasn't until the back door opened and a middle-aged woman of featherweight size entered the kitchen that she realised how far the morning had progressed.

Lang's introduction confirmed her assumption that this was Jessie Verdon, but as soon as she had responded to the older woman's greeting Nicole promptly felt the heat of embarrassment sweep into her face as she remembered just what she was wearing and imagined the conclusions their apparent cosy tête-à-tête could have given rise to.

'Well, I—I guess I'd better collect my clothes and be going. Dad will probably be waiting for me,' she half smiled self-consciously and began edging towards the laundry. And to Lang, 'Thank you for—for taking the time to explain those procedures for me. It—er—makes things much simpler when you know what's going on.'

'You're welcome,' he drawled, watching her discomfited withdrawal with every evidence of amusement before turning to his housekeeper to explain, 'Nicole fell in the pool, hence her state of déshabille while her clothes were being dried.'

'Oh, did you, dear?' Jessie tutted sympathetically. 'How annoying for you!'

'Yes, it was rather,' Nicole's flashing eyes glared pointedly in Lang's direction, then she shrugged, 'Still, these things happen.'

Once dressed and feeling more secure in her own clothes, Nicole hung her borrowed raiment on the back of the bathroom door and prepared to thank Jessie for her help, as had been her original intention.

'Think nothing of it, dear, it was no trouble,' her appreciation was waved aside equably a while later. 'If it gave you more time to be out and about with your father, then I'm pleased. I think he misses your company more than he cares to let on.'

'Mmm, then I'd better not rob him of any more of it than I have to,' Nicole smiled, and indicated her bare feet. 'I still have to collect my sandals from down by the pool. I'd forgotten all about them till I went to get changed. Oh, and could you say goodbye to Lang for me, please, when he comes back?' There hadn't been sight nor sound of him since she left to get dressed.

'I can certainly do that if you like, although he shouldn't be long. He only went to answer the phone.'

'Yes, well ... I'm sorry, but I really think I ought to be going. I'll catch up with him some other time, I expect,' she evaded, already making for the door.

'All right, dear, off you go, then. I'll tell him,' Jessie called after her.

Lang's soaking towel was still lying where he had thrown it in disgust when Nicole reached the pool and it was an automatic gesture for her to wring it out and drape it over the step rails to dry. Her sandals were just as easy to locate but a little more difficult to recover. One was on the edge where she had left it before testing the water, but the other was at the bottom of the pool, having been dislodged during her fall. Looking about her for a garden implement—a rake, or something similar—with which to fish it out, she could see nothing suitable and stood staring down at it in annoyance. She had no intention of going back and asking Lang for his assistance.

The idea occurred to her that as it was the shallow end she just might be able to reach it with her toes if she lowered herself over the side as far as possible without actually letting the water reach to her shorts. But after several unsuccessful attempts she once again found herself wishing she was taller. It was so frustrating to be able to get so close without actually being able to touch it. Her elbows were starting to complain about supporting her weight on the pebbled edge too, and with one last exasperated grimace— there was nothing for it but to go back to the house and ask for help after all—she began inching herself slowly upwards.

By pushing her feet against the wall she eased herself sideways so she could get one hand to the ground in place of her elbow, but when something light and spindly crept over her arm she instinctively went to shake it away and so doing lost her grip and slid gently, but unavoidably, into the water up to her waist. The sight of a pair of long drill-clad legs passing her vision as she slipped downwards didn't improve her disposition at all, and neither did the glimpse of Lang tossing a twig of belah away.

'You did that deliberately, you miserable rotten louse!' she hurled at him furiously, her hands tightening into fists as they came to rest on her hips. 'You intended this to happen!'

'One good turn deserving another?' he drawled, eyes dancing.

'Except that in my case it *was* an accident ... as I kept telling you! Only you're too damned biased to have realised it!'

'I wonder why?'

His eyes were so sceptical and his voice so dry that Nicole reddened self-consciously. In all truth she couldn't really bring herself to blame him entirely for his disbelief. Her attitude towards him hadn't been exactly been guaranteed to breed trust.

'Well, there was still no reason for you to do this,' she protested resentfully, easily scooping up her sandal with her foot now. 'I still think it was a pretty crummy thing to have done.'

One corner of his mouth tilted obliquely. 'I hope you're not expecting an apology.'

'From the omnipotent Lang Jamieson? Hardly!' It was her turn to look wry now. 'I'm not that much of an optimist!'

'Never mind, kitten,' he laughed aggravatingly as she pushed herself up on to the side of the pool—without his help this time. 'Knowing the way your militant little mind works, I'm sure you'll find some irritating way to exact retribution for all those imagined injustices of yours.'

Imagined? He had to be joking! But how right he was when he said she would be finding some way to get her own back, and the sooner the better, to Nicole's indignant way of thinking.

The opportunity presented itself more quickly than she could ever have wished. When she walked towards him in order to collect her other sandal he obligingly bent to pick it up for her and while she accepted it in her right hand as he was rising, her left hand reached out to push against him as hard as she possibly could.

The result was satisfying in the extreme. When he surfaced he was as livid as she had been five minutes earlier.

'I hope you're not expecting an apology,' she used his own words against him with a delighted chuckle.

Her gratification, however, wasn't sufficient to make her stay and brave the full force of his wrath.

The ominous look on his face as he surged through the water to the side was enough to have her swallowing nervously and flying for the path before he could fulfil the punishment his eyes only threatened. In fact, she didn't slow her expeditious retreat until she reached the front fence of her father's cottage, and only then because a swift glance over her shoulder showed no sign of pursuit. At a more leisurely pace she continued on into the house.

'What on earth have you been up to?' Her father took in her wet shorts and breathless state wonderingly.

A quick look back towards the door—she was still half expecting Lang to materialise behind her—and she laughed shakily, 'Oh—er—nothing much. I was trying to get one of my sandals out of the pool when I—er—slipped in, and I hurried all the way home in case you were waiting on me.'

He didn't appear particularly convinced. 'And might I ask how your sandal came to be in the pool in the first place?'

'It just ... fell in,' airily.

'Out of your hand, I presume?'

'No, while on my foot—I was wearing it at the time,' she confessed with a rueful grin.

Bryce closed his eyes for a moment and then eyed her suspiciously. 'Would you mind please explaining?'

Nicole shrugged and spread her hands wide. 'It's

quite simple really,' she began, and made it so by conveniently omitting Lang's share of the dampening mishaps. She didn't care to remember what had happened after the first, and she was certain her father wouldn't have approved of the second.

'Actually, the most embarrassing part was when Jessie came into the kitchen and found me looking as if I'd been there all night,' she continued quickly before he had a chance to question her.

'Oh, that wouldn't have worried Jessie,' he laughed.

Her eyes widened sarcastically. 'You mean she's used to coming home and finding half-dressed females sharing his breakfast table?'

'No,' he sighed exasperatedly. 'I mean that, unlike the habit you seem to have developed concerning Lang, she wouldn't be jumping to the wrong conclusions without waiting for an explanation.'

Nicole hunched a defensive shoulder and decided it was time to get changed. She was doubly glad now she had decided against telling him the whole story. He definitely wouldn't have approved of that last indulgent impulse!

CHAPTER SIX

THE remainder of the weekend passed all too swiftly and almost before Nicole had time to realise it, her father had driven her back to town and it was Monday again.

Gervaise was late for his swimming lesson that afternoon, strolling into the pool as if he had all the time in the world and Nicole had nothing more to do than wait on his convenience. He took an age to get changed and when he did finally emerge from the dressing rooms it was to stop and chat to a school friend before ambling towards her.

'You're sure you're ready?' Nicole couldn't help the dry enquiry when he had actually made it to her side. He was going to make her late for her regular swimmers if he dallied any longer.

'Mmm, I think so,' he replied self-assuredly. 'What are you going to show me first?'

'Nothing to start with,' she smiled. 'I think the best idea would be for you to show me what you can do first of all.'

He shrugged and pointed to the shallow end of the pool. 'There?'

'If you like.'

'I can do all the strokes,' he informed her matter-of-factly as they walked to his chosen spot. 'My mother took me over to Franklyn for a coaching clinic last year.'

Personally, Nicole doubted that the attendance at one clinic would have been sufficient to have taught him each style. Still, she mused, a lot did depend on how enthusiastic and apt a pupil he had been. She would reserve judgment until she had seen him perform.

And perform, she was to decide later, had been exactly the right description! He appeared to know the mechanics of the strokes well enough, but getting him to produce them in the water was something else again. At one stage she even began to suspect he was being deliberately obtuse. Never had she come across a child who did so many things wrong so continually. It wasn't even as if he didn't have the intelligence to interpret her instructions because he certainly had that all right, but whatever she asked of him he seemed to do the opposite.

When she said to pull his free-style stroke through with a bent arm beneath his body, he pulled straight down by his side. If she told him to blow all the air out under water he came up spluttering and complaining he couldn't get another breath. His head came higher when she wanted it lowered, and he dragged his legs like leaden weights instead of using them as she suggested. His handling of the other strokes was no better either. If something could be done wrong, he did it.

Eventually, after what Nicole privately considered must have been the most frustrating coaching period of her life, she called him over before he left to get dressed.

'Gervaise, do you really want to learn to swim?' she questioned, watching his reaction closely.

'My mother says it's very important that I be able to swim.'

'Which is quite true, of course,' she agreed. 'Although that wasn't really what I asked. I enquired whether *you* wanted to learn.'

His expression told her nothing. As on Saturday, the aloof gaze was unwavering. 'I couldn't join the Swimming Club otherwise, could I?'

'And you want to join it?'

'My mother says. . . .'

'Yes, yes,' she cut across him rapidly. Good lord, did he prefix all his statements with those three words? 'But what do you say?'

His eyebrows peaked as if she had just said something slightly foolish. 'Lang Jamieson's the President, isn't he?'

'So?' Nicole's brows went winging this time.

'He's a very strong swimmer.'

'I'm still not sure what that has to do with your wanting to become a member,' she puzzled. Somewhere, somehow, she seemed to have lost track of this conversation!

'He takes an interest in me.'

Because he's going to marry your mother? Nicole almost asked aloud, but managed to stop herself in the nick of time. Saying instead, 'I see. You mean it was Lang who suggested you should join?'

'No,' he shrugged. 'It was my mother.'

Nicole ran a hand through her hair and decided to cut her losses. This was getting her nowhere.

'Oh, well, providing your mother agrees, and you really want to do competition swimming, you'd better come down and see me again tomorrow afternoon,' she recommended. 'We've got a lot of hard work ahead of us to correct those actions of yours.'

'That's what I thought.'

For one incredible instant Nicole thought she detected a tiny thread of pleasure at the prospect in his voice. However, a closer inspection of his expression showed she must have been mistaken. His demeanour was as dispassionate as ever.

The following day was a complete reversal, weather-wise, with wind and rain making the conditions so unpleasant that, because of lack of patronage, Rod closed the pool soon after lunch. Nicole had spent most of the morning compiling the time sheets for the Club's races on Wednesday evening, sorting out the nominations for the various events, and generally getting some paperwork done. In that regard,

a respite from her normal heavy schedule had been
quite welcome and opportune.

Now, as she bade goodbye to Rod, she ducked her
head low against the continuing downpour and with
a quick look in both directions darted across the road
to the paddock. Beneath the sheltering trees she
paused for a moment, her attention returning to a
familiar vehicle she had fleetingly noticed parked in
a driveway further along the street. Of course, her
train of thought moved onwards after having her first
impression confirmed, she should have expected to
see Lang's Falcon outside Eunice Blanchard's house.
They were going to marry, weren't they?

It was a strangely disquieting thought and one
which started a dull ache in the region of Nicole's
midriff, although she couldn't really understand why
it should. Lang was nothing to her, never would be,
never could be. These thoughts didn't relieve the
subtle pain either and she shifted restlessly. She knew
she should have moved on, but some intangible force
kept her where she was until a slight movement beside the front door had her stepping backwards in
order to see more clearly. It was Lang, and she surmised he could only have arrived seconds before she
crossed the road because he appeared to be waiting
for someone to answer the door.

When it was eventually opened it was flung wide by
a tall, raven-haired woman dressed in a stylish silk
blouse and flaring red velvet slacks. The distance was

too great for Nicole to see her features properly, but it was obvious who she was by her reaction to her visitor. Long silken-clad arms reached out to encircle Lang's neck and pull his head down to a cherry-red mouth which met his in a long devouring kiss.

Nicole about-faced and began running across the paddock. The ache inside her increased to a burning shaft of pain which she put down to her own self-disgust at having stopped to watch such a passionate reunion. She should have known better than to have stayed. What had she expected them to do ... shake hands?

Much to her discomfort the scene she had witnessed was still vivid in her mind when Earl returned from school later in the afternoon and, on the spur of the moment, she accepted his offer to go out to dinner with him that evening. She had refused on the two previous occasions when he had invited her, but tonight she felt the need for company and a chance to set her thoughts along less disturbing paths. A nice meal, a little wine, and some amiable conversation seemed just the right thing.

They went to the Roman Room, an Italian restaurant and the best of the two in town, where they ordered *saltimbocca*—delicious wafer-thin slices of veal and smoked ham topped with a leaf of sage, then rolled and served with saffron rice and leaf spinach— and an excellent bottle of Chianti. The faultless cuisine, together with the wine, certainly helped

Nicole to relax physically, but her mind perversely remained emotional. Provoking images kept recurring and in her attempts to shut them out she often shut Earl out too. When, for the third time since beginning their meal, she heard his voice break in on her private contemplations she looked across the table at him with a contrite gaze.

'I'm sorry, Earl, I'm not very good company this evening, am I?' she smiled regretfully.

The glance he gave her was warm and encompassing. 'I'm not complaining.'

'Then you should be. It's hardly what one expects from a dinner companion.'

'I figured you might have been worried about your squad missing their training this afternoon when the first races are due to be held tomorrow.'

'Oh, no, it won't hurt them,' Nicole shook her head quickly. 'They'll still do okay.'

'Any budding champions?' he grinned.

'Well, I wouldn't exactly go that far,' she laughed back. 'But I do think there's definitely a couple there with the ability to do very well if they persevere with it.'

'Why didn't you?' he now wanted to know. 'You're good enough.'

'Not really,' she disallowed wryly. 'Besides, I was always more interested in the theory of swimming rather than the practice. Oh, I thoroughly enjoy the swimming I do these days, but I must confess that

when I was in training at school I used to find it just
a little bit tedious. All those miles looking at a black
line underneath the water!'

'At least it didn't give you an over-developed
figure,' he complimented her.

'No, well, it does some and not others, I guess,' she
avoided his admiring gaze self-consciously. 'But
enough of me, what about you? How did you come to
be interested in coaching?'

Earl shrugged and grinned. 'Much the same way as
you did. I'd always liked the sport, although I was
never much good at it competitively. "Great style, but
no pace," as one of my instructors was fond of saying,' he laughed. 'Then, having completed my studies
to become a teacher, it just seemed a natural exten-
sion of my job to help out at the local pools wherever
I've been posted. I like working with kids, they're so
adaptable.'

'Mmm, aren't they?' Nicole agreed enthusiastic-
ally, and then frowned as she remembered one in particular who had been anything but!

'What was that for?' Earl queried, seeing the
creases in her forehead. 'Did I say something I
shouldn't have?'

'No, of course not,' she smiled away the furrows. 'I
was just thinking of Gervaise, that's all.'

'Oh, and what's he been up to?'

'Nothing really, it's just that when he came for his
lesson on Monday it was almost as if he didn't want

to learn anything. I've never come across a child of his age before who consistently gets *everything* wrong. Usually they begin to show an improvement in at least one aspect of their style.'

'Well, I shouldn't worry about it too much if I were you,' Earl advised consolingly. 'He's deep, that one, though I think half his trouble is that he's been taught to expect preferential treatment because of the family's social standing and connections, and when he doesn't get it he's at something of a loss.'

An observation Nicole couldn't quite be persuaded into believing. At no time had she seen Gervaise Blanchard display any sign of losing his assured composure.

'Surely that wouldn't apply in this instance, though?' she pressed, 'After all, he is having private lessons—he's not one of a squad. How much more preferential can you get?'

'Hmm, I see your point.' He pulled at his lip thoughtfully and then hunched his shoulders. 'In that case, why don't you do a complete reverse and suggest he join one of the classes and see what effect that has?'

Nicole's expression was distinctly rueful. 'I tried that on Saturday, but after coming to the conclusion that I was never going to get past the "My mother says," barrier, I gave in gracefully. Personally, I think he would do much better in a group. Most of them pick the idea of it up from each other like smoke.'

'Yes, they're great little copyists, aren't they?'

After that their conversation returned to less enigmatical subjects—the schools where Earl had taught, amusing anecdotes respective to their occupations, their families, and a host of general topics.

When they left the restaurant the rain had ceased, although the roads were still wet, but the clouds were clearing in the inky sky to allow the diamond shine of a few stars to appear, and they decided to walk home instead of catching another taxi. It wasn't far to the Guthrie house and the air was cool and fresh after the rain, scented with the perfume of spring flowers.

Outside her bedroom Earl drew Nicole into his arms to kiss her tenderly, and she didn't resist. He had been a comfortable and undemanding companion and she felt a trifle guilty through having used him in an effort to block out her own problems. His gentle lips evoked no uncontrolled response from her, though, and when she stepped back out of his hold she felt no emotion at all apart from a calm friendliness.

All during Wednesday Nicole was on edge, wondering whether Lang would put in an appearance at the pool that night. His presence, as President, wasn't strictly necessary on race nights, of course, and as he lived so far from town she wouldn't have been surprised if he didn't come. Nevertheless, if he did arrive it would be their first meeting since Sunday morning and she wasn't exactly anticipating the encounter with a great degree of confidence. He could no doubt, if he so chose, make things extremely unpleasant for her in a number of ways. Luckily, though, her time would be occupied the whole evening by marking down each swimmer's times and there wouldn't be an opportunity, she hoped, for a confrontation to take place. If she hadn't had this thought to sustain her, she knew she might even have been coward enough to chicken out altogether by feigning illness and spending the whole night in her room in order to avoid him for that little bit longer. .

As it was, she was too busy ticking off the children's names against their point-scoring attendance records, and handing out stopwatches to timekeepers, to even be aware when he actually arrived. Her initial realisation came when she looked up from the clipboard in her hand to see his commanding figure some yards away, his back to her as he spoke to one of the officials. Biting her lip, Nicole hurriedly bent her head to her work again and stayed that way until the very last name was entered.

The orange lane markers were in place and over the microphones Rod Barker was already summoning the first eight competitors to their blocks when Nicole hurried down to the thirty-metre mark. It was a heat of the novice event and she was anxious to see how Rhonda Parrish fared. From the time they left the blocks, however, till the moment they touched the finish line, there was never any doubt as to who

was going to win the race. Rhonda's dive was sure
and true—the only aspect Nicole had been nervous
about—and her stroking sound. Discovering she had
outpaced the rest of the field by a good five metres,
Rhonda's face broke into a wide ecstatic smile and
she waited eagerly for the others to finish so she could
hear her time. Nicole swiftly made a note of all the
finishing times for the various lanes and then the
children were called out of the pool.

'What time did I do, Miss Lockwood, what time
did I do?' came Rhonda's excited questioning immediately she had clambered up the steps.

'Twenty-seven point four seconds,' Nicole smiled
down at the spirited face. 'Which wasn't a bad effort
at all. You won't be allowed back in that distance
again,' drily.

'I don't mind,' came the happy exclamation. 'I
want to do the longer distances.'

That unquenchable enthusiasm again, Nicole
smiled, and then lowered her gaze to the sheet again
as the others crowded around her wanting to know
how long they had taken to cover the distance.

The evening wore on with race following race in a
well organised pattern and Nicole was pleased to see
the rest of her squad fulfilling her hopes and expecta-
tions as the events progressed. It was also gratifying
for the children themselves to be so satisfactorily rewarded for all the time and effort they put into their
training.

At no time had Nicole actually come face to face with Lang, although she had been nervously aware of his presence a couple of times when walking to the starter. Mostly, he kept to the opposite side of the pool and Nicole was thankful to have it so. As soon as the programme was finalised and the equipment returned to the storage room it was another matter, though. A large proportion of the children and their parents had left by then and as the last of them were filing out through the gateway so Rod could lock up she had no choice but to acknowledge his existence.

'Good evening, Lang,' she called in as coolly moderate a tone as she could manage, but still keeping in step with Earl. He had been one of the time-keepers for the night.

'Good evening, Nicole,' Lang returned from where he was conversing with a man she didn't know, a touch of dryness in his voice. 'I have a message for you from your father, so don't go yet, will you?'

Damn him! she scowled explosively. She should have just nodded and kept walking!

'It's all right, Nicholls, I'll see her home safely afterwards,' Lang continued with a dismissive glance in Earl's direction.

'There's no need,' Nicole positively glared at him. How dared he order her escort around! 'I'm sure whatever Dad asked you to tell me won't take long.'

'Longer than you're imagining, obviously,' he rapped back immediately.

With a heavy and disgruntled sigh she turned to the man still waiting patiently beside her. 'Perhaps it will take longer than I expected, Earl.' But definitely no longer than was absolutely necessary, she fumed. 'I'm sorry, but I'll see you later. Okay?'

Apparently Earl saw nothing untoward in the request because he shrugged agreeably and said, 'Sure —I'll have the coffee all ready made and waiting by the time you arrive.'

'Lovely,' she seconded the idea. 'I could do with a cup, I didn't have time for one after dinner.'

'My pleasure,' he winked and, offering a sketchy salute to Lang and his companion, started off across the road.

An introduction proved Lang's heavy-set associate to be the Club treasurer, Clive Waterhouse, but as they were discussing unfamiliar matters Nicole lost interest, glancing about her discontentedly. They were the last ones left and it was taking forever for them to finish their conversation. She would have thought they could have chosen a more appropriate time to discuss the advantages of silage—whatever it was! At last they showed signs of moving and it was with gratitude that she said goodnight to the older man.

'You're sure you can spare me the time?' she immediately turned to enquire sarcastically of Lang.

'Only with a superhuman effort,' he retaliated in like manner. 'But if you're not interested in hearing what your father asked me to pass on....' His voice tailed off significantly and he made as if to head for his car parked on the other side of the street.

'Oh, no, you don't!' She determinedly planted herself in front of him. 'Having kept me waiting this long, you're not going to walk off now without telling me!'

'Who's going to stop me? Nicholls? You forget, he's gone to make the coffee so it's "all ready and waiting for you",' he mimicked harshly. 'How very obliging he is!'

'Which is a damned sight more than can be said of you, so don't start making fun of Earl because he happens to treat me decently,' she flared.

'Decently! What's that supposed to mean? That he considerately makes you coffee and then suggests you go to bed together?'

'No!' she cried vehemently, shaking with rage. 'But even if he did, it wouldn't be any concern of yours! You're nothing to me, Lang, nothing!'

Her nerves had been strung tightly all day and now, coupled with the indefensible power he had to play on her emotions, the combination was proving too much for her self-control and, whirling, she raced across the road with tears beginning to stream down her cheeks. As she passed his car she could hear his closing footsteps behind her and spun to face him, her breath coming fast and shallow, her fingers clenching.

'Leave me alone, Lang, just leave me alone!' she choked. 'I'm not interested in listening to any more of your disparaging insinuations, or your self-made rules detailing how I should behave. So please, just go away and allow me to live my own life!'

'And leave you in this state?' he grated roughly, two hands coming up to cradle her head between them, his thumbs brushing away the tears. 'Nicholls will think....'

'Who cares what Earl thinks? Who cares what any man thinks? I hate the lot of you!' she sobbed brokenly. 'And don't touch me!' trying to jerk out of his hold. 'You're all a load of two-faced liars, only interested in your own egotistical aims.' Then, when he didn't release her, 'I said don't *touch* me!' as she began pummelling violently at his broad chest.

'For God's sake, Nicky!' Lang gripped her wrists grimly in one hand and wrenched open the car door with the other. 'Get in,' he muttered, and bundled her flailing figure on to the back seat. Slamming the door behind them, he pinned her helplessly to his muscular form until she had exhausted her struggles and consented to stay there, crying quietly.

When her tears finally stopped, Lang bent his head to look at her watchfully. 'Okay now?' he probed.

Nicole sniffed and nodded, easing herself away from him embarrassedly. 'I'm sorry,' she murmured throatily but refusing to return his gaze. 'I guess I made quite a fool of myself, didn't I?'

'No, but it's still fairly obvious someone's hurt you badly. You think of him a lot, don't you, kitten?'

Oh, yes, I still do that, but only as a last restort to get you out of my mind, she replied to herself. Aloud, she softly admitted, 'Sometimes.'

Lang exhaled deeply and brushed her rumpled hair back from her flushed face with a gentle hand. 'He isn't worth it, you know,' he sighed.

'No, he isn't,' she agreed shakily, her nerve ends alive and trembling at his touch. At last she turned to face him, her deep blue eyes anguishedly seeking his. 'Lang, I. . . .' The remainder of the words stuck in her throat at his expression and she licked at feverishly dry lips. 'Oh, Lang!' she whispered defencelessly when his arms began to pull her back to him.

At first his lips met hers softly, comfortingly, but her response to the tantalising pressure was so unconditional that they quickly became more ardent. His hands swept down the arching curve of her back and she melted against him, her whole being crying out for his possession. It seemed she had thought of almost nothing else but this man since the day of their meeting, and the heavy thud of his heart beneath her exploring fingers showed he wasn't indifferent to her either.

With a muffled moan of disappointment she felt his lips leave hers and trace a sensuous path down the side of her neck to the throbbing base of her throat as his hand slid the zipper of her velour jacket down to her waist. In a desire-filled daze she watched unprotestingly as he unclipped her front fastening bra and swept it aside, her pink-tipped breasts abandonedly pressing against his caressing hands.

'God, but you're beautiful,' he mouthed huskily against the tender swelling curves, and making Nicole shiver with the unexpected force of the feelings he was so effortlessly arousing.

She didn't know how she could have been so unsuspecting as to have fallen in love with him after the farce Jerome had made of that emotion, but she had all the same. Of that she had no doubts. But as love was synonymous with marriage in Nicole's mind it was only a matter of seconds before her thoughts had jumped from one subject to the other with shocking results. Lang was planning to marry Eunice Blanchard! Hadn't she seen with her own eyes sufficient evidence yesterday to corroborate his intentions in that direction? The recollection was like a stinging slap in the face and Nicole went rigid with shame and mortification. How could she have forgotten so easily again and allowed him such freedom?

Lang's head lifted to hers immediately he felt her previous quiescence turn to resistance. 'What's wrong, Nicky?' he puzzled.

'Nothing.' She eased herself gently but stiffly out of his hold, fumbling to re-fasten her clothes. 'I stupidly—but only temporarily, I'm glad to say— forgot my own well-founded observations, that's all,' she replied through trembling lips.

He made no attempt to stop her, but his eyes narrowed alertly. 'Which are?'

'Yes, I suppose it was convenient for you to forget too, wasn't it?' she gibed.

'Forget what?'

'That you're no different from any other man,' she retorted. 'That you're all natural double-crossers, wanting to have your bread buttered on both sides!'

A hand on her arm gave her a good shake. 'What the bloody hell are you talking about?' he demanded coldly.

Nicole twisted her arm free with a strength born of humiliation and anger. 'I told you before, Lang ... don't touch me!'

'It's a little late to be giving that particular order, isn't it?' he drawled, his expression insufferably mocking.

A crimson stain tinted Nicole's cheeks and her disdain faltered, but only briefly. She was well in control of her emotions the next time their eyes met.

'As to what I was talking about....' She shrugged and sent him a scornful glance. 'Well, if you want to play ignorant that's quite okay by me, but you needn't think I'm going along with it just to cater to your masculine vanity. Not this girl!' Her voice rang with conviction as she pushed open the door and hurriedly stepped out. 'You can sweet-talk your way around some other female for that questionable pleasure!'

Without giving him a chance to reply, or even

waiting to hear if he had one to offer, she slammed the door shut and stormed across the paddock with her back straight and her head high. Appearing cool on the outside, she felt raw and lacerated on the inside.

The most galling part of the whole episode had been her unqualified surrender to Lang's lovemaking. That she should have readily submitted—no, welcomed it was far more honest, she confessed painfully—was something she found impossible to accept. The only thought left to salvage at least some of her pride being the knowledge that Lang wasn't aware how deeply her feelings were involved. Her humiliation was bad enough now, but it would have known no bounds if she had inadvertently revealed how she really felt about him.

CHAPTER SEVEN

It wasn't until Nicole was at work the next morning that she realised she still hadn't received the message her father had entrusted to Lang and at lunch time she rang the cottage, hoping to find him at home. When it wasn't answered she remembered him telling her that during the week he had most of his meals at the homestead and she hung up. She would try again that evening, and keep trying until she did catch him at home. She had no intention of phoning the main homestead and running the risk of Lang answering the call.

Fortunately she managed to get through to Bryce a couple of hours after dinner and as soon as they had exchanged greetings, somewhat surprised ones on his part, she went on to answer his query as to why she was ringing.

'Lang—er—said he had a message for me from you last night, but he didn't ...' she paused, biting her lip, 'actually get around to telling me what it was.'

'It was nothing to cause a panic,' he laughed. 'Just that I would be picking you up on Saturday, the same as I originally intended last week, and driving you back here for the weekend.'

'Is that all?'

'Why?' She could almost see his frowning look. 'Were you expecting something else?'

Nicole ran his fingers distractedly through her hair and clenched her teeth together tightly. Of all the ...! She could have screamed! To think that the whole of last night's devastating experience could have been avoided was too much to bear. From the way Lang had spoken she had been convinced he'd had something more important to relay. As, no doubt, he had fully intended her to believe, she seethed smoulderingly.

'No, no, not really,' she answered her father's question at last, managing to sound normal only with an effort. 'It's just that I thought—that I thought you might have heard about our first swimming carnival this Saturday and were going to invite yourself along with us to Franklyn,' she improvised rapidly. Up until that moment she had completely forgotten all about it herself.

Bryce chuckled good-humouredly. 'Not me, love, unless you're competing, of course. You know how I feel about that sort of thing. That's all in your line, not mine. I take it I won't be seeing you on Saturday, then,' he continued.

'No, I'm sorry, not if you won't come with us.' A sudden thought occurred and she put it forward tentatively. 'Do you know if—if Lang will be coming?'

'I shouldn't think so,' he vetoed the idea calmly,

much to Nicole's relief. 'He's expecting visitors on business this weekend. They've come down from the north to see about buying some breeders.'

'I see,' she nodded gratefully. 'How about Sunday, will you be free then?'

'As far as I know.'

'Well, it wouldn't be worth a double trip for only one day, so why don't I see if I can find someone who's going that way to give me a lift, or, alternatively, why don't you drive in and we can spend the day seeing the local sights,' she suggested brightly, hoping he would choose the latter. The less she visited Yallambbee the less likelihood of her running into Lang.

'Which particular local sights are you referring to?' Bryce quizzed wryly.

Nicole tut-tutted admonishingly. 'Don't sound so sceptical, there are quite a few as a matter of fact. I've been making enquiries for just such an eventuality,' she told him with a laugh. 'I'm told there are some rather spectacular limestone caves on the road back to the ranges which are well worth a look. Then, of course, there's the National Park for bush-walking or trail riding, and Ida was telling me the other day that there's a very good spot a few miles down river if you'd like to do some fishing ... and you know you do,' she added slyly. 'Would you like me to continue?'

'No, I think that's enough to be going on with,' he returned drily. 'Which of the three do you fancy?'

'You're the one who's having to make the trip, you decide,' she offered generously, then went on to say, 'I'll see to the food and the bait.'

Bryce broke into amused laughter. 'You obviously know me too well, young lady, but perhaps we'd better wait and see what the day is like before making a final decision. The weather is still a little unpredictable at this time of year.'

'You mean, like Tuesday? Mmm, it was pretty miserable, wasn't it?'

Their arrangements sorted out, Bryce rang off shortly afterwards and Nicole headed slowly for her room, mentally going over what had been said. She couldn't ever remember a time before in her career when she had forgotten a coming carnival quite so swiftly, or so entirely. She had always prided herself on the standard of her work and the sincere interest she took in it, and she didn't intend to allow one man to destroy that dedication now. If it took forever she would manage to put him out of her mind somehow! She had done so with Jerome, hadn't she?

Much to Nicole's pleasure the carnival turned out to be quite a success for the Nullegai swimmers. Not that they managed to take out any of the finals— except for Marilyn Barker, Rod's daughter—but they did fill a few places in the heats and most of them bettered their previous times. In a few months it was possible that with a continued rate of improvement, which was a definite probability considering their ages and lack of experience, they could be pressing stronger claims against competitors from other Clubs before the end of the season.

As the weeks passed the weather grew hotter and on her trips out to Yallambee Nicole could see the acres of wheat ripening to a golden yellow beneath the burning rays of the sun and knew that it wouldn't be long before the giant combines moved in to begin their systematic harvesting of the matured grain. On these visits to her father's cottage she made certain she stayed well clear of the homestead in order to have as little contact with Lang as possible.

She usually saw him each Wednesday at the race meetings, but their encounters were of a very brief duration and her manner was always cool and aloof. Lang's feelings were somewhat harder to determine. He was always civil, impassive almost, and Nicole could only assume that he cared neither one way nor the other whether they were on speaking terms or not. He had succeeded in putting a brake on her goading comments and she supposed that had been as far as his interest went.

From her point of view it was a satisfactory outcome in that, due to the sparsity of their communications, her involuntary antagonism had all but faded. In its stead, however, and nowhere near as satisfactory, was an emotion far harder to dispel—a love, unwanted by either of them, reflected Nicole mirthlessly, which at times threatened to overwhelm her

with its intensity. She had thought that with their
paths crossing so rarely it would, after a while, have
died a natural death through lack of nourishment.
But this, apparently, wasn't to be. By Tuesday of
each week she was certain she was as indifferent as
Lang was, but then Wednesday night would come
around with monotonous regularity to prove how ex-
travagantly she was deluding herself. Her feelings
were as strong as ever and showed no signs of abat-
ing.

In an attempt to bury the aching pain she perpetu-
ally carried she threw herself into her work with a
restless enthusiasm. Often she remained at the pool
long after she was needed, or was required to, and
although her pupils gained tremendous benefit from
these extra hours, Nicole did not. She began to lose
weight noticeably. So much so that Rod was forced
to remark upon it and suggested she cut down on her
ever-increasing work load.

To a certain extent she did as he advised, but as she
privately considered the enjoyment she attained from
her work more than compensated for the loss of a
few pounds in weight she continued much as before.
There was only one mark against her record so far—
Gervaise Blanchard. No matter how long she spent
with him demonstrating and instructing he really
couldn't have been said to have improved. Some
afternoons Nicole was sure there were glimpses of an
imminent breakthrough, but by the next day they had

disappeared again and she was back where she started. It was frustrating to say the least!

One afternoon she was surprised to see Gervaise attend his lesson accompanied by his mother. Although she had heard a considerable amount about Eunice Blanchard from others, Nicole had never met her and while Gervaise used the dressing rooms she watched the older woman's approach warily. Dressed in a layered dress of fashionable pink silk, a wide-brimmed white hat seated on her severely styled hair, she looked exactly what she was—wealthy, sophisticated, arrogant. Also a trifle out of place, Nicole added, to boost her own morale.

From her superior height Gervaise's mother eyed the girl before her with haughtily raised brows. 'Don't tell me *you're* the coach!' she opened the conversation disparagingly.

Nicole gritted her teeth, but answered politely. 'I'm Nicole Lockwood, yes. Is there something I can do for you, Mrs Blanchard?'

'Ah, you know who I am, then?' She appeared inordinately pleased at the thought.

There was an uncontrollable twitch to Nicole's lips. Now she knew who Gervaise had copied his attitude from. 'I presumed—when I saw you arrive with Gervaise,' she replied.

'You hardly look more than a schoolgirl yourself.' The dark eyes were minutely assessing and dissecting. 'I understood you were supposed to be qualified.'

'And so I am,' Nicole defended promptly, although she couldn't entirely blame Eunice for the comparison. With her hair in its normal pigtails to keep it out of the way, she didn't really consider she presented a credible picture of adult womanhood. 'My certificates and letters of recommendation are in the office if you would care to check them.'

The suggestion was discarded with a supercilious sniff. 'There wouldn't be much point. If you're not able to pass on what you've been taught, they're worthless, aren't they?'

'And you're worried that I might fall into that category?'

'Oh, no, not worried, Miss Lockwood ... convinced!' was the scornful retort. 'How could it be otherwise? My son tells me you haven't been able to teach him anything since he's been coming here.'

Nicole's cheeks burnt at the charge of incompetence but, at the same time, she reluctantly had to admit that she didn't have the results to disprove it.

'No, well, I'm afraid he's not altogether wrong,' she had to confess. 'However, I do feel he might find it easier if he was allowed to join one of the classes instead of continuing with individual tuition. A lot of children can't....'

'Are you trying to shift the blame for your own shortcomings on to my preference for private lessons?' Eunice laid an affected hand on her chest to interrupt in a disbelieving voice.

'No, of course not!' Nicole disclaimed with a frown. 'But I am of the opinion that....'

'Quite frankly, Miss Lockwood, I'm not the least bit interested in your opinions,' Eunice broke in again contemptuously. 'All I wish to hear is whether you can, or cannot, teach Gervaise to swim correctly. If you can't then please have the goodness to say so—thereby ceasing to waste my money and my son's time, and enabling me to find someone who *is* capable of teaching him!'

'Naturally, that's your prerogative, Mrs Blanchard,' Nicole confirmed stiffly. 'But if you would have the goodness to allow me to finish a sentence, I would like to point out that I've come across difficulties similar to Gervaise's before and in the majority of cases they've made great advances when put among other children.'

'Majority of cases, Miss Lockwood?' Up went those cleverly pencilled eyebrows again.

'That's correct, Mrs Blanchard, majority of cases,' Nicole determinedly stood her ground. 'Unfortunately some children are almost impossible for anyone to each because they're just not interested in learning! I'm sure you recall the saying, "You can lead a horse to water, but you can't make it drink".'

Eunice's ruby red lips curved sarcastically. 'How fascinating! And such a handy excuse for all your failures.' The satire suddenly gave way to knife-edged steel. 'Of course my son wishes to swim well. He wants Mr Jamieson to be proud of him.'

More evidence of Lang's interest, Nicole noted miserably.

'You mean, Lang wouldn't be, if Gervaise couldn't swim?' she made herself ask.

'However *Mr* Jamieson feels is no business of yours, Miss Lockwood!' Eunice snapped summarily. 'We were discussing my son! Now, do you have the ability to teach him or shall I take him elsewhere?'

With her professional credibility at stake it was Nicole's turn to take the offensive. 'If, as you maintain, Gervaise does want to improve, then yes, I believe I have the ability, Mrs Blanchard,' she returned icily. 'But it will have to be on my conditions, not yours. From now on he joins a squad and practises with the others.'

Eunice nodded abruptly. 'All right, Miss Lockwood, you may have your conditions. I just hope, for your sake, they happen to be successful, otherwise I'll have you sacked on the spot. I command a great deal of influence in this town, don't forget.'

'I'll keep it in mind,' Nicole owned drily, and eyed the woman in distaste as she took her leave, smiling condescendingly at Rod as she flounced past the kiosk.

After a week with the squad, to Nicole's sighed relief, Gervaise appeared to be progressing nicely— slowly, it was true, but there definitely had been some headway. Then, for no obvious reason that Nicole could see, he slipped backwards again. Not only that, but worse, he started to become a disruptive influence with the rest of the swimmers. He ducked, pushed and splashed until Nicole thought she would go out of her mind, and the other children began complaining bitterly that he was ruining what had been an enjoyable part of their day.

'I really don't know what else to try!' She flung her hands wide in defeat as she walked home with Earl after one particularly irritating session. 'He started to improve and then, bingo!' she snapped her fingers in the air, 'he's back to being hopeless again. Honestly, I've never met another child who's reacted quite like he has.'

Earl's solution was short and to the point. 'I'd give him up as a bad job, if I were you. No one expects you to achieve a hundred per cent success rate.'

'His mother does,' she recalled ruefully. 'She said she'd have me fired if he didn't improve.'

'Lovely woman!' Earl slapped angrily at a bush as they passed. 'That's the sort of remark I'd expect her to make.' A few more steps and he encouraged, 'Not that I think she could do it. The Committee would have to have some say, surely.'

'I wouldn't know.' Nicole hunched her shoulders dismally. 'Maybe, if they're her friends, they would take her view.'

Silence reigned while they both considered the disquieting possibility.

'Would you like me to take him in my squad for a while and see if that helps?' he offered obligingly.

Nicole shook her head and smiled faintly. 'No, thanks, Earl, it wouldn't be fair to your swimmers if you had to spend all your time with Gervaise.' Earl helped with the more advanced members of the Club, those who needed conditioning rather than style coaching.

'What will you do, then?'

'I would like to try and have a talk with him, but the minute I start to ask a question about his swimming he shuts up like a clam and gives me one of those unblinking stares of his,' she half laughed. 'Meanwhile, I guess I'll have to continue as before and hope for the best. There's not much else I can do.'

'I suppose not,' he sympathised soberly, then brightened to suggest, 'Unless you can get Lang Jamieson to have a word with him instead. I've heard rumours that he and the redoubtable Mrs B. might be getting together shortly. It's worth a try, don't you think?'

'No!' she gasped, horrified. Ask Lang to intercede with her problems? Not likely! 'I mean to say, can you imagine how it would look, the coach crying on the President's shoulder because she can't get one eleven-year-old to swim properly!'

'Mmm, it wouldn't exactly inspire confidence, would it?' he sighed.

Another two weeks went by without Nicole coming any closer to solving her problem. Two weeks in which she had had to endure another acrimonious visit from Eunice Blanchard who had come to check for herself on her son's progress, or lack thereof. On the following Friday there was to be another Club meeting and as Eunice had informed her of her intention to be present with the parting threat, 'And don't doubt that I won't be there, Miss Lockwood,' Nicole wasn't particularly looking forward to the evening.

It wasn't surprising, therefore, that she was preoccupied all day Friday. And not only with thoughts of her own troubles but also with disappointment at having been unable to get through to Gervaise. She hated to see any child incapable in the water and it had always given her a tremendous sense of satisfaction to see each pupil well on their way to becoming a competent swimmer and know that she had prevented the probability of that child becoming a drowning statistic.

As each one of her squad finished their last lap and automatically checked their times against the pace clock at the end of the pool, Nicole sent them off to change and then waited for Gervaise, the last, naturally, to complete his modified work-out. At last he made it to the steps and pulled himself out.

'Okay, Gervaise, that's it for today. You can get dressed now,' she said. 'Mr Barker will be closing up in a few minutes.'

He nodded and began moving away, only to turn back after a few steps. 'Miss Lockwood?' He glanced at her uncertainly.

'Yes,' Nicole answered in some surprise. It was the first time she had ever seen him the least bit indecisive.

He seemed uncomfortable—another first—but his words were clear enough. 'My mother says she's going to have you fired because of me. Is that true?'

'Yes, well, I gather she's going to try,' she admitted ruefully.

'I'm sorry, it wasn't your fault.'

'It wasn't yours either, Gervaise, so don't let it worry you. We just couldn't find a suitable wavelength, that's all.'

'But it is my fault,' he contradicted dogmatically. 'You see, I thought that if—that you ...'

'Mmm, you thought I would...?' she prompted gently, her interest fully aroused.

'Tell me to get lost if I was bad enough,' he divulged in a rush.

'So you were doing it on purpose!' Nicole wasn't angry at his deception, she was relieved. Her dismal failure to improve his style had begun to have her seriously doubting her own ability. 'But why didn't you tell me when I asked you if you wanted to learn? It would have saved us both a lot of wasted effort.'

'But if I told you, my plan would have failed, you see,' he explained miserably. 'You would have told my mother the truth.'

'Instead of which, I was supposed to play the heavy and get you off the hook by throwing you out, is that it?' wryly.

'Sort of,' he hunched one shoulder awkwardly. 'Mother said I *had* to be able to swim well enough to compete for the Club.'

'Which, I presume, you're not interested in doing.'

'Not really. I wanted. . . .'

'Yes. . . ?' she tried to ease it out of him again.

'To play tennis,' he revealed, downcast.

It seemed unbelievable to Nicole that all her trouble should have originated through his desire to play another sport. 'Why can't you play tennis if you want to?' she queried in bewilderment.

The look Gervaise gave her was a speaking one, as old as time itself.

'Lang Jamieson isn't the President of the Tennis Club,' he informed her drily.

Nicole couldn't believe her ears. 'You mean, all this has been brought about through wanting to impress *Lang*?'

'Just about,' he agreed with unruffled calm. 'Only I didn't mean it to turn out this way, Miss Lockwood. I didn't know my mother would take it out on you,' in a more troubled tone.

'Oh, well, maybe it's not too late to save something from the mess,' Nicole reassured him with a smile and started moving towards the kiosk. 'Can you swim correctly, by the way?'

A red flush of discomfiture showed beneath his skin. 'Better than I have been doing,' he disclosed, embarrassed.

Nicole felt happier than she had done for several days. 'After this business is cleared up, would you come back and show me how well?' she invited.

'If you want me to,' his agreement was readily given. 'I like swimming for fun, but not for training,' he grimaced, and as they neared the end of the pool, 'I really am sorry for the trouble I've caused you, Miss Lockwood, and—and for being so hard to get on with.' A sigh and he went on thoughtfully, 'My mother says I should learn to make people do as I want, that I'm entitled to it because of our family's position in Nullegai ... but you don't make many friends that way, do you, Miss Lockwood?'

'No, you don't, Gervaise,' she rumpled his hair sympathetically. It was a hard lesson for one so young to have to learn, but it probably wouldn't do him any harm for all that. 'It makes it much easier, and nicer, for all of us if we try to co-operate instead of dominate.'

'Somehow, I don't think Mother would agree,' he grinned suddenly.

To Nicole's mind the effect was quite startling. Like a chrysalis being transformed into a butterfly, Gervaise had changed from a rather haughty-looking child into an engaging one.

'Perhaps not,' she smiled with him, but refrained from adding anything further. It wasn't her position to openly criticise his parent to his face. 'But now ...' she paused and looked down at him wryly, 'we come to the burning question. Who's going to be the one to tell her about all this? Do you want to do it, or would you prefer me to?'

Gervaise swallowed hard and stared down at his feet. 'I think I'd better.'

'You're sure?'

'Yes,' he glanced up quickly and nodded. 'I caused it, so I should be the one to tell her.'

A very brave decision, thought Nicole as she saw him into the dressing rooms and then joined Earl and Rod who had been waiting at a discreet distance while she talked with the boy. His mother wasn't exactly going to be filled with maternal love and affection when she discovered just how, and why, he had been duping them both.

The Club meeting was held in the local community hall and Nicole was pleasantly surprised to note the number of interested persons present. It was good, and augured well for the Club, that so many of them had taken the time to attend. Lang was there, of course, sitting at a desk on the dais at the end of the hall together with the other office bearers, and looking heart-constrictingly attractive in a short-sleeved safari suit of chocolate brown and a cream open-necked shirt.

Nicole tried to make herself as inconspicuous as possible and took a seat on the far end of one of the middle rows. She had only just taken a notebook and pen from her bag, in case there were any remarks she needed to remember, when Eunice Blanchard arrived. Tonight she was wearing slim-fitting slacks and a blazer style in white linen and, amidst effusive greetings to those she considered worthy of acknowledgment and freezing looks of disdain for those she didn't, she made her way to an aisle seat near the front.

At precisely eight o'clock the meeting was called to order, the apologies noted, and the preliminaries dealt with. Nicole listened with interest to the correspondence and the minutes of the previous meeting being read, and made a few notes of her own as relevant points were touched upon. Then as soon as the treasurer's report had been accepted the meeting was thrown open for general discussion.

No sooner had the invitation left Lang's lips than Eunice was on her feet, causing Nicole to wonder what else she had found cause to complain about beside herself.

'Mr President, members of the Committee,' her voice rang out, imperiously demanding their attention, 'I would like to move a motion of no confidence in Miss Lockwood, our newly appointed coach, on the grounds of gross incompetence, and suggest a replacement for her be found forthwith!'

While Nicole sat too stunned to move—hadn't Gervaise said anything to his mother, after all?—and a sea of eyes turned in her direction, Lang spoke from the chair.

'Before this matter proceeds any further, Eunice, perhaps you could tell us in what way you consider Miss Lockwood has failed in her undertaking,' he invited.

Eunice was back on her feet before all the fascinated faces could swing towards her again. 'In every way, Mr President!' she declared with a touch of the dramatic. 'My son has been attending the pool for instruction from Miss Lockwood for some weeks now. Initially, for private tuition, and recently, against my judgment I might add, in a class. In all that time his swimming not only hasn't improved in the slightest, but it has decidedly and noticeably deteriorated! It is my opinion that the girl has clearly over-stated her proficiency in this field—the evidence of my son is there to verify it—and I believe she should be discharged without further delay in order to avoid a repetition with any more of the children who have been unsuspectingly exposed to her misguidance!'

A moment of utter silence as Eunice sat down again and then Nicole could hear Lang's voice asking impassively, 'Miss Lockwood, would you care to answer Mrs Blanchard's charges?'

'Yes, thank you,' she murmured, and rose shakily
to her feet, her fingers clutching at the chair in front
of her. The vindictively worded attack had left her
shocked and bewildered. 'In my defence I would just
like to say that—that I believe. . . .'

'Mr President!' Eunice's voice cut furiously across
her explanation. 'I have moved a motion for Miss
Lockwood's dismissal and I would like to hear you
call for a seconder. We are not required to listen to
any fabricated excuses for her inadequacy in the
meantime!'

'Oh, shut up, Eunice, and let the girl have her say,'
advocated a tall fair-haired man impatiently in the
row behind her. 'We've heard your side of the story
and I for one would now like to hear hers.'

Eunice swung round on her seat to glare murder-
ously at him. 'I'm quite within my rights to ask for it
to be seconded,' she hissed. 'And don't you dare tell
me to shut up, Bob Maher, or I'll. . . .'

'*Order!*' Lang demanded in a tone that cut like a
whip. And having successfully gained the quiet he
called for, 'You have the floor, I believe, Miss Lockwood?'

'Thank you,' Nicole acknowledged his query
throatily. 'As I was saying, I believe that in Gervaise's
case there happens to have been a conflict of interests.
Although he attended the lessons, he didn't like
swimming training and hoped, by appearing to get

worse, to be thrown out of the class in order that he might play another sport. One that he does enjoy,' she concluded pointedly.

An inelegant hoot of laughter issued from Eunice's throat. 'It's surprising you didn't think to mention that to me when I spoke to you only two days ago, Miss Lockwood!' she jeered.

'Probably because I only discovered the true facts myself this afternoon, Mrs Blanchard,' Nicole retaliated swiftly. Now that she was recovering from her original feeling of numbness she was determined not to submit tamely. If she was going down, she would be going down fighting!

'This afternoon?' the other woman repeated scornfully. 'When I had already intimated to you what I would be suggesting to the Committee tonight? Do you honestly expect us to believe such a fantasy?'

'Yes, I do, since it's the truth,' Nicole defended her statement stoutly, even though she realised that, in the manner Eunice had represented it, it did sound somewhat improbable.

'I can vouch for that!' someone suddenly called out from the back of the hall and, turning round, Nicole saw Earl rising to speak on her behalf. 'Nicole and I have discussed the difficulties she was experiencing with young Gervaise on a number of occasions, but it's quite true that it wasn't until this afternoon that she found out what's been troubling him,' he corroborated her defence.

Even over the ensuing buzz of interested comments Eunice's malicious denunciation sounded clearly.

'Of course, you *would* support her fanciful tale. The pair of you probably share the same bed as well as the same boarding house!'

The buzz now became a muted roar as indignant protests and recriminations flowed back and forth across the hall. Nicole clamped down on her bottom lip in an angry kind of despair and sent Earl a warning shake of her head. It wasn't fair that he should be on the receiving end of Eunice's venomous tongue as well!

It needed Lang to call the meeting to order again so they could proceed. But not before he had cautioned,

'I shouldn't advise you to let your personal grievances overcome your common sense again, Eunice, or it's possible you could find yourself the defendant in two suits for slander and defamation of character.'

Incensed at having been publicly rebuked, Eunice almost spat her next demand. 'Then would you mind putting an end to this ridiculous charade by calling for someone to second my motion ... as I originally asked? The girl obviously has nothing but preposterous excuses to make!'

Envisagaing her career in ruins with such a black mark against it, Nicole made a last-ditch stand. 'Mr President!' she called urgently. 'May I ask a question of Mrs Blanchard?'

Lang turned enquiringly to Eunice, who nodded with an assumed boredom. 'Oh, ask whatever you like,' she exhorted mockingly. 'Only don't take too long about it, otherwise we shall still be here at midnight.'

'I'll certainly try and get it over with as quickly as possible.' Nicole fought hard to control her escalating temper. It was her whole career the woman was preparing to wreck so callously and, putting her faith in a young boy's promise, she plunged on. 'My question is just this. Could you please tell me why you still feel it necessary to carry out the threat you made some time ago to have me sacked, since Gervaise told you this afternoon, the same as he told me, exactly why he hadn't been making any progress?'

'Can you prove that?' Lang rasped above the new outburst of noise.

'N-o,' she was forced to admit dismally. 'But Gervaise said. . . .'

'Of course she can't prove it!' Eunice interrupted with a sneer. 'Because there's nothing to prove, that's why! Can't you see that all these little references hinting that Gervaise didn't want to learn to swim are a cover-up for her own ineptness? Why on earth would I have gone to the trouble of paying for his lessons if he didn't want to go?'

It was the answer Nicole had been hoping for and she seized her opportunity with both hands. 'Oh, I know the answer to that one, Mrs Blanchard,' she retorted, and allowed her eyes to slide insinuatingly towards the dais and back again. 'Only I didn't think you would care to have it made public!'

'You know nothing about...'

'Are you calling my bluff, Mrs Blanchard?' This time it was Nicole who interrupted, her voice deadly serious, her eyes unwavering.

Two red stains flared across Eunice's cheeks and her dark eyes glittered vengefully. It was obvious she would have liked to, but didn't quite dare. Eventually she scraped back her chair in a furious motion and whirled to her feet.

'You little...!' She broke off then as if only suddenly aware of being the cynosure for all eyes and, with one last vitriolic glance at Nicole, stormed down the aisle and out of the hall.

Her departure left a dumbfounded void which Bob Maher quickly filled.

'Mr President,' he began. 'Since Eunice has seen fit to—er—withdraw her charges, I feel the Club owes Miss Lockwood an apology for having been subjected to such unfounded accusations.'

His suggestion brought forth such a rousing chorus of agreement that Nicole exclaimed embarrassedly, 'Oh, no, please, I'm just grateful I was able to disprove Mrs Blanchard's allegations. The Club doesn't owe me an apology.'

She received one anyway, delivered by Lang on behalf of all those present and accompanied by a round of applause at the finish. It was such a heart-warming recognition of her innocence that Nicole felt tears prick at her eyelids and had to blink them hurriedly away. She had succeeded in winning the battle; now was not the time to cry.

The rest of the meeting was an anti-climax. Matters were discussed and dealt with quickly and efficiently, and in less than an hour the books had been closed and everyone was preparing to leave. Nicole waited by her chair for some of the crowd to disperse, but on looking up to find Lang heading unerringly towards her, she skipped around one group of people and swiftly made her way to Earl's side and the open doorway.

As President he'd had little choice except to agree with the other Club members, but Nicole didn't doubt he was far less pleased with her victory over Eunice Blanchard than she was!

CHAPTER EIGHT

'OH, Dad, it was awful! I've never felt so mortified in all my life!' Nicole exclaimed next morning on the way to Yallambee after narrating the previous night's events for her father's information. 'The woman was absolutely malevolent, and I still can't understand why! I've never done her any harm that I know of.'

'Well, I shouldn't worry about it too much, if I were you.' Bryce reached out to pat her arm consolingly. 'You've been cleared of all her spiteful charges, and that's the main thing.'

'But it leaves such a bad taste.' She wrinkled her nose in dissatisfaction. 'I feel as if from now on everybody will be secretly watching what I'm doing just to make sure for themselves.'

'That's ridiculous,' he laughed. 'You received a public apology, what more do you need to convince you they've dissociated themselves from Mrs Blanchard's accusations?'

Nicole shrugged and smiled faintly. 'I suppose you're right. I wish it hadn't happened, though, all the same.'

'Stop worrying! You've got the whole weekend ahead of you and by Monday everyone will have forgotten all about it, you'll see.'

Forgotten by everyone except Eunice and Lang, she meditated morosely. It would be a long time before either of them forgot about it. She turned towards her father with the same question on her lips that she asked each Saturday.

'Will Lang be there this weekend?'

This time, however, his reply was the exact opposite of what she had come to expect.

'No, he flew out with Clive Waterhouse and Bob Maher this morning to attend a cattlemen's conference in Tamworth, and they're not expected back till some time Monday.'

On a happy sigh Nicole leant back in her seat, visibly relaxing. Now she could really enjoy her two days off. She had been dreading the thought that she might come face to face with Lang during this particular visit to Yallambee. She needed time, a lot of time, to prepare herself for the verbal assault she anticipated receiving from him at their next encounter. His comments regarding her showdown with his future bride would be savagely cutting, she was certain!

As had become the custom on her visits, Nicole and her father had lunch soon after they arrived at the cottage and then, saddling two mounts, spent the afternoon riding over the property. By now there wasn't much of it that she hadn't seen and although she enjoyed their rambles along the hot river flats, it was their excursions into the hills that she liked the best.

There it was a virtually undisturbed wildlife sanctuary where native flora and fauna abounded and the unusual and the unexpected became the norm. The sight of a pert-faced wallaby darting away into the undergrowth, a quill-encrusted echidna burrowing his long snout into the earth in search of food, or the sound of a lyrebird—superb in song and mimicry—never lost their fascination for her and each time they returned it seemed her father pointed out something new.

During the evenings they usually read, played Scrabble, or watched television, depending upon their inclinations at the time. It was a complete change of environment for Nicole and she slipped into it easily. She was even beginning to understand, and to share, her father's fondness for his somewhat isolated way of life. She had to admit it did have its compensations.

Sunday was a scorcher. From horizon to horizon there wasn't a cloud to be seen and the blinding light from the sun had stripped the sky of almost every vestige of its colour before they had even finished their breakfast.

'What are we going to do today?' queried Nicole while squinting through the window at the glare outside as she did the washing up.

'I don't know about you, love, but I'll be spending

most of my time patrolling the property. With this dry spell we've had, any fire that gets a hold today will spread like a raging inferno,' Bryce answered sombrely.

'Couldn't I come with you?'

'Uh-uh!' he disagreed. 'I'll have a couple of the hands to help me and it won't be a very pleasant day riding around in this heat. No, you go on up to the homestead and keep cool by having a swim. If there's anything happening Jessie will be the first to know with the two-way radio.'

'I still don't see why I can't go with you. The heat doesn't bother me and surely another pair of eyes is always welcome,' she argued persuasively.

'We'll be taking the bikes, Nicky love, not the horses.'

'So?' She couldn't see what difference their mode of transport made.

'Well, for a start, that would mean you would have to ride pillion, right?' And after her agreeing nod, 'Which straight away doesn't give me the advantage of another pair of eyes at all, seeing we would be in the same place at the same time and not covering any extra ground as you implied.'

She hadn't thought of that. 'There's still nothing to stop me from using a horse, though, is there?'

'Nothing, that is, except me,' Bryce smiled drily, but returned to his serious mien immediately afterwards. 'Listen, Nicky, you've never yet seen a bushfire but, believe me, they're not something you treat lightly! Not only do you not know the property well enough for me to allow you to go out on your own, but there've been occasions when even the fleetest horses haven't been capable of getting people out of trouble. There only needs to be a wind spring up behind a fire and it will run across the ground and up trees so fast you wouldn't believe your eyes if you saw it!'

Nicole's expression was wry. 'In other words, I'm staying at home,' she quipped.

'Sorry, love, but it really is the best place for you on a day like this,' he commiserated gently. 'You go on up and have a swim like I suggested and keep Jessie company. I expect she'll be glad to have someone to talk to with the rest of us away.'

'Okay, okay, I can take a hint as to when I'm not wanted,' she pulled an ironic face which set him laughing.

Any other weekend and Nicole would have refused point-blank to go up to the homestead, but the knowledge that Lang was away put the matter in an entirely different light. So, after donning an orange and green flowered bikini beneath her halter top and shorts, she started up the well-worn track shortly after her father had left.

She called in on Jessie first and was grateful for the long cool glass of lemonade she was provided with as they shared a companionable hour in the kitchen. Even the relatively short walk from the cottage had brought forth beads of perspiration as the sun's relentless rays had seemed to penetrate through her skin to her very bones. Her father had been right, she was finally forced to concede. Unless it was absolutely imperative, today wouldn't have been the best of days to be out riding.

Later, when Nicole suggested she might use the pool, Jessie was all motherly concern.

'You mind you don't stay in that water too long, then,' she warned. It's hot enough out there to fry you all the way through.'

'Don't worry, I'll be careful,' Nicole smiled back reassuringly. 'I have no wish to lose the tan I've got by turning it into a mass of blisters.'

'And use one of the loungers in the shade of the bushes over there,' Jessie continued with a wave of her hand towards the covered walkway. 'If there's a breeze at all you'll catch it best in that position.'

Nicole promised to do as she suggested and after leaving her outer garments in the downstairs bathroom made her way across the terrace to the inviting patch of blue. She had decided against wearing a cap and had already plaited her hair as she usually did for work before leaving the cottage. This time she didn't bother to test the temperature but kicked off both sandals at the edge and dived straight in.

After the blazing heat it was gloriously refreshing and she back-stroked the length of the pool in sheer delight. For a while she merely floated on her back, blissfully calm and serene, but when the strength of the sun on her face couldn't be denied any longer she rolled over and began to free-style leisurely.

In between drowsy rests on the lounger she spent the greater part of the morning in much the same fashion. Jessie came out once to tell her that Bryce had called in on the two-way to advise that, so far, all was safe and well and that there was so signs of anything untoward developing. Nicole had thanked her and lightly proposed that she join her, but Jessie had declined with a chuckle and gone back to the house declaring, 'Good old terra firma is where I belong.'

The drone of a bee very close at hand had Nicole flicking her eyes open to ascertain where he was and, seeing him hovering over her exposed midriff, she prudently decided it was time for her to head back to the pool once more.

She hadn't been in long and was idly back-stroking again when she ran into something solid and two hands grasped her about the waist. Her muffled squeal of surprise was cut short when she was lifted and spun around into a pair of encircling arms.

'Lang!' she gasped in both protest and astonishment. 'What are you....'

His descending mouth stilled her words, although definitely not her heartbeat, and as it was too deep for her to stand she had no choice but to cling to him for support. Nevertheless, the instant he raised his head she rounded on him angrily.

'And just what was that for?' she demanded.

One corner of his shapely mouth quirked indolently. 'Aren't I entitled to charge a fee for the use of the pool?' he teased.

'Not that kind, I'd rather pay in coin,' she retorted, trying unsuccessfully to squirm out of his hold. 'What are you doing back here anyway? I thought you were supposed to be gone until Monday.'

'And instead I return early to find you're certainly not averse to using the pool while I'm away. Normally, you couldn't be persuaded to come within a hundred yards of the homestead, could you, Nicky?' he enquired with coolly mocking overtones.

Of course not, the thought that I might have run into you was too disturbing for my precariously balanced emotions, she answered miserably to herself. For Lang she had a totally different reply.

'A circumstance which I've no doubt pleases you better too, so if you will kindly let go of me I'll take myself back to the cottage without further delay.'

'Oh, no, you don't!' His arms tightened relentlessly when she again attempted to break loose. 'I haven't finished with you yet.'

'Then, if it's not too much bother, of course, would you mind if we move to shallower waters?' she queried sarcastically. 'I feel at a distinct disadvantage being out of my depth like this!'

'I prefer it.'

'Well, I don't!' She pushed against his bare chest furiously but ineffectually. 'And if all you want to do is to censure me because of what happened the other night then don't bother, I'll save you the trouble. I'm sorry I put your lady love's nose out of joint, but she didn't really leave me any option. It was my *career* she was proposing to demolish so casually!'

'I was well aware of that, but for your information Eunice Blanchard does not happen to be my lady love, as you put it,' he informed her roughly. 'We may have been seen together a number of times since her husband died because she asked for my help and advice in dealing with the estate, but apart from that there's absolutely nothing between us!'

'Liar!' Nicole almost shouted in her anger at his duplicity. 'I happened to see the two of you on her porch one afternoon as I was on my way home from the pool, and the manner in which she greeted you sure didn't suggest it was a platonic relationship to me!'

'In that case, perhaps you should have waited around a little longer and then you would have seen me firmly detach myself from that same unwelcome greeting, because I certainly had no intention of returning it,' he advised with a decided bite in his voice.

'Says you!' she scoffed recklessly. 'That's not the way I've been hearing it.'

'I don't give a damn what you've been hearing!' His fingers dug deeper into her waist. 'Eunice means

nothing special to me and never has. I made that clear
to her some weeks ago when she looked like persuading herself differently.'

Nicole still didn't know whether to believe him or
not. 'Well, what about the other night, then? I noticed it was all *Eunice* this, and *Eunice* that! While
what was I? The inconsequential *Miss* Lockwood,
made to remember she was the outsider of course!'
she accused stormily.

Amber eyes were raised skywards in exasperation.
'You damned little idiot, what in hell have the names
I used got to do with anything? Of course I called her
Eunice, I've known her ever since I can remember
and I've never called her Mrs Blanchard in my life!'
he stated categorically. A hand beneath her chin
turned her face up to his and he continued in a softer
vein, 'But you weren't the outsider, Nicky, take my
word for it.'

Beneath her long curling lashes Nicole's gaze was
still troubled. 'If I hadn't been able to prove my story
she would have found someone to second her motion
and I would have been out on my ear without you
lifting a finger to stop her,' she complained forlornly,
without stopping to rationalise that she hadn't really
given him any reason to wish for her retention.

'I wouldn't have had to,' he smiled.

'Wouldn't have wanted to, you mean!'

'A word of warning, kitten,' Lang lowered his head
fractionally in emphasis. 'You got away with calling

me a liar once today, I wouldn't push my luck and try for twice, if I were you.'

The feel of his hard length pressed against her in such a prolonged contact was making Nicole desperate to break away.

'Why, what will you do? Deprive me of your scintillating company and let me go?' she taunted with insolently wide eyes.

For a moment she thought he meant to wring her neck, but then the brilliant fire went out of his eyes and his grip loosened.

'Perhaps I'd better,' he said flatly. 'While I still can.'

Now that she was able to move away Nicole found she wasn't as eager to leave as she had believed. 'While you still can?' she queried, half puzzled, half wary.

It was he who had started to move away, but now he turned back sharply. 'That's right, you provocative little...!' He bit off an uncomplimentary denunciation and began pushing through the water towards her, making her back away nervously. 'You may be able to set my adrenalin pumping faster than any female I've ever met, but I'm damned if I'm going to let you kill me by inches while you amuse yourself playing advance and retreat as and when the mood takes you!'

Kill him by inches? Astonishment brought her to a standstill. Did he mean what she thought he meant?

She began to speak slowly, fearful of a misunderstanding on her part.

'Are you saying...?'

'That I want you—yes! That I love you—that too!' His eyes held hers challengingly, but she thought she detected a slightly husky tone to his voice. 'But then I guess that's what you always intended. You were determined someone was going to pay for Jerome's treatment of you, and who better than me? After all, I've been a convenient substitute right from the start, haven't I?' he charged harshly.

'No ... anything but, actually,' she denied with a radiant smile, her heart feeling as if it would burst with happiness at his revelations. 'You were too damned overpowering to stay that far in the background. Every time I thought of Jerome an image of you would supplant itself over the top of him.'

His lips curved satirically. 'That must have been distressing for you!'

'Yes, it was rather,' Nicole agreed, and lowered her head slightly to slant him an impish look. 'But what's even more distressing is the fact that I'm standing here with the man I love to distraction—and who says he loves me—but all he wants to do is waste time throwing ill-founded accusations at me.' Closing the gap between them, she slid her arms around his neck and gazed up at him adoringly. 'Would it be asking too much for you to kiss me instead?' she murmured.

Lang clasped her to him convulsively, his lips already half way to hers. 'I'm sure that can be arranged,' he groaned deeply.

Their embrace was long and fervent and Nicole revelled in the feel of his hard body strained against hers, the touch of his hands as they caressed her bare skin. His mouth moved temptingly over hers and she responded uninhibitedly, pressing even closer to his lithe frame and sliding her fingers tantalisingly over the smooth flesh of his strongly muscled back.

Slowly, Lang's lips left hers to travel lightly, captivatingly, across velvety cheeks to the vulnerable side of her arching throat and the tender curves of rounded breasts. Yielding to an increasing passion, Nicole returned his amorous explorations freely, using her own soft lips with seductive persuasion by tracing a delicate pattern along the side of his taut jaw and across bronze shoulders. With the shuddering release of a long breath Lang cupped her face between his two hands to hold her captive.

'When?' he demanded thickly. 'When are you going to marry me? To be able to touch you like this but not have the right to take you to bed with me is nearly driving me crazy! For God's sake, make it soon, kitten!' he groaned.

Nicole turned her head slightly to press a gentle kiss to the palm of his hand. 'Whenever you say, my darling,' she glowed. 'In case you haven't noticed, you're not exactly a calming influence on my emotions either!'

'I hope not,' he smiled so slowly that her heart pounded raggedly against her ribs. Then, laying an arm across her shoulders, he tucked her close to his side, urging drily, 'Come on, let's get out of here. It certainly never occurred to me that, when the time came, I would be doing my proposing in the middle of a swimming pool.'

'For me, I guess it was appropriate,' Nicole grinned.

'There are quite a few things I would consider appropriate for you, my love,' he drawled lazily as he lifted her on to the edge and then agilely pulled himself out of the water. 'Not the least of which is a good hiding for implying that I was attempting to make you feel an outsider on Friday night.'

Accepting his hand to help gain her footing, Nicole glanced upwards reproachfully. 'I could have been fired for all you seem to care,' she pouted.

'By whom?'

'Well, by Eunice and—and whoever supported her, naturally!'

'And who would that have been, do you think?'

'How should I know?' She stared at him in amazement. 'From the stony way you kept surveying me all evening, it might even have been you for all I was aware.'

'I was furious with myself for not being able to put

you out of mind,' he revealed ruefully.

'And what better way to do that than to get me put out of the district altogether!'

'You really are a blind little idiot, you know that?' Lang gazed into her upturned face with amused disbelief. 'Don't you realise, even yet, that there wasn't a single person in that hall—and that definitely included me, if you still happen to have any doubts on that score—who would have supported Eunice? I've had nothing but your praises sung to me for the work you were doing and the results you were achieving ever since you started at the pool. Believe me, Eunice's was a lone voice crying in the wilderness where your likely dismissal was concerned.'

Nicole flushed with pleasure. 'I wish I'd known that, then I wouldn't have needed to worry so much about the likelihood of my never seeing you again,' she sighed. 'I may have avoided you all these weeks, but only because it hurt too much to be near you when I believed you intended marrying Eunice Blanchard.'

'So now you know how I felt about you being seen so constantly in Earl Nicholls' company,' he countered wryly.

'Don't tell me you were jealous ... of Earl!' She couldn't believe it.

'If I wasn't, then I hope to God I never have to experience that particular feeling again!' he retorted forcefully.

'But—but there was no need for you to be,' she protested earnestly. 'I told you once before, if you remember, that it wasn't by my invitation that he was always with me. We shared the same interests, nothing more.'

'But given enough time, people change,' he commented heavily. 'Once you were in love with Jerome.'

'I *thought* I was, I know differently now,' she corrected him softly. 'What I felt for Jerome was nothing compared to how I feel about you.'

It was the right answer and Lang rewarded her in the nicest possible way—a kiss which demonstrated all too clearly the depth of his feelings in return. When they parted Nicole tilted her head to one side, her expression shyly quizzical.

'When did you first think you might be falling in love with me?' she asked.

'The night we met,' drily.

Her mouth formed a perfect circle of surprise. 'But you couldn't have! I—we...' a deepening colour invaded her suddenly hot cheeks and she continued hastily, 'you didn't even know what I looked like!'

'No, but I knew what you felt like,' he smiled reminiscently. 'You were crying so hard in your sleep that it seemed the most natural thing in the world to turn you into my arms in an effort to give you some comfort. Then, when I kissed you with the same purpose in mind, you returned it so ardently I suddenly found myself wishing you had meant it for me.'

'You said you only did it because I was disturbing your sleep,' she reminded him chidingly.

'Yes, well, you were certainly doing that,' he owned with an unrepentant grin. 'I was torn between an inexplicable desire to either keep you protectively close beside me, or to go and find whoever had hurt you so badly and flatten him!'

'I wish I'd known that too,' Nicole smiled wistfully. 'Maybe then I wouldn't have been quite so antagonistic towards you.'

'Which, in turn, might have precluded the need for you to work yourself so hard.' He ran his hand experimentally down her side from midriff to hip. 'You've lost weight, kitten,' he reproved.

'I had to try and keep my mind occupied with something other than you. But there's no need to worry, I'm sure I'll put it back on again now. In fact,' she eyed him teasingly, 'I shall probably become quite fat and contented—just like one of your cows.'

Lang shook his head in mock sternness. 'I'll have you know, my cows happen to be prime ... not *fat*!'

'Oh, dear, I've still got a terrible lot to learn, haven't I?' Nicole somehow managed to look suitably chastised. 'I thought I was paying you a compliment.'

'I can think of others I would rather have,' he returned drily, the look in his gold-flecked eyes causing her heart to miss a beat.

'You weren't, by any chance, thinking of anything

in the unspoken line, were you?' she questioned with a twinkle.

'You know damned well I was,' Lang retorted huskily, and caught her to him possessively, his lips meeting hers hungrily.

Nicole clung to him unreservedly. The time for talking would come later. At the moment she was only interested in demonstrating how much she loved and needed this man.

Harlequin Romances

The books that let you escape
into the wonderful world of romance!
Trips to exotic places...interesting
plots...meeting memorable people...
the excitement of love.... These are
integral parts of Harlequin Romances –
the heartwarming novels read by
women everywhere.

Many early issues are now available.
Choose from this great selection!

Choose from this list of classic Harlequin Romance editions.

MEDICAL ROMANCES

Relive a great love story...
Harlequin Romances 1980
Complete and mail this coupon today!

Harlequin Reader Service

Please send me the following Harlequin Romance novels. I am enclosing my check or money order for $1.25 for each novel ordered, plus 59¢ to cover postage and handling.

☐ 449	☐ 528	☐ 658	☐ 804	☐ 904	☐ 451
☐ 454	☐ 532	☐ 711	☐ 805	☐ 911	☐ 462
☐ 464	☐ 538	☐ 712	☐ 856	☐ 918	☐ 468
☐ 469	☐ 557	☐ 730	☐ 861	☐ 409	☐ 478
☐ 494	☐ 597	☐ 766	☐ 890	☐ 430	☐ 485
☐ 500	☐ 604	☐ 796	☐ 892	☐ 438	☐ 489
☐ 513	☐ 627	☐ 800	☐ 895	☐ 443	☐ 491
☐ 516	☐ 643	☐ 802	☐ 901	☐ 446	☐ 495

Number of novels checked @ $1.25 each = $_____

N.Y. State residents add appropriate sales tax $_____

Postage and handling $_____ .59

                        TOTAL $_____

I enclose _____
(Please send check or money order. We cannot be responsible for cash sent through the mail.)

NAME _____
                      (Please Print)

ADDRESS _____

CITY _____

STATE/PROV. _____

ZIP/POSTAL CODE _____

Offer expires September 30, 1980.   00456426100

What readers say about Harlequin Romances

"Harlequin books are so refreshing that they take you into a different world with each one you read."

"I hope Harlequin goes on forever."

M.Z. Hollywood, California

"Harlequin books are great; once you start reading them, you always want to read more."

T.E. Ogden, Utah

"Harlequin books bring love, happiness and romance into my very routine life."

N.J. Springfield, Missouri

*Names available on request

JOY
ROMANCE
LOVE

Harlequin
Omnibus
THREE love stories in
ONE beautiful volume

The joys of being in love...
the wonder of romance...
the happiness that true love brings...